"Remo. Remo. Remo." hissed, like the soundtrack from a nightmare of horror and death.

He knew the direction the sound came from now, but the gusting, whistling winds still made it difficult to pin down the source.

It was slow work. Five yards forward. Was the sound louder? No? Then back five yards, and move off five yards in another direction. Slowly, he saw that the sound was taking him farther and farther from the A-frame. And still the same single name being called, over and over: "Remo. Remo. Remo." He was getting close now, close enough to know that the voice was the practiced, whispering hiss of someone, probably a man, trying not to let his voice be recognized.

He looked through the darkness of the night but saw no one. He heard no movement, no unusual sound except his name, muffled, being called again and again.

It was getting much louder now. He knew he should be almost on top of the caller. But still he saw nothing. The sound seemed almost to come from below his feet.

He looked down but before he could inspect the snow he stood on, there was another sound, a strong whooshing sound. He looked up, back across the hundred yards, toward the back of the A-frame.

In horror, he saw flames burst from the rear windows of the A-frame. He started to run, but he had taken only three steps when the cabin lodge exploded before his eyes.

And Joey and Chiun were inside.

THE DESTROYER SERIES:

The Destroyer #42

Warren Murphy

TIMBER LINE

PINNACLE BOOKS   LOS ANGELES

THE DESTROYER #42: TIMBER LINE

*Copyright © 1980 by Richard Sapir and Warren
Murphy*

An original Pinnacle Books edition, published for the
first time anywhere.

First printing, November 1980

ISBN: 0-523-40716-5

Cover illustration by Hector Garrido

Printed in the United States of America

PINNACLE BOOKS, INC.
2029 Century Park East
Los Angeles, California 90067

For Chrissie, and the Eternal House of Sinanju
P.O. Box 1454
Secaucus, NJ 07904

Timber Line

CHAPTER ONE

The younger man did not sweat. Even here in the steamy, putrid depths of a Matto Grosso night, the younger man did not sweat.

That is what Karl Webenhaus hated most about him. He hated it even more than the fact that Roger Stacy was noisily, joyously making love to Webenhaus's wife in the open-flapped tent next to his. He hated the non-sweating even more than the fact that Stacy was going to kill him and claim for himself all the glory and the money from the discovery of the magic oil tree, which Webenhaus had worked and struggled and sweated after for so long. Roger Stacy had never sweated after anything. That was what Webenhaus hated most about him.

Webenhaus stretched and groaned. He put down his fountain pen and got up from the camp table and stretched again. His report was done.

He stretched one last time, then scratched his ample stomach. Fifteen years ago, he thought, that stomach had not been there. Fifteen years ago, he had been beautiful. So had Helga. She still was; but he wasn't, not anymore.

And why should he be? First, there had been all the long years of sabotaging Hitler's Third Reich while pre-

2

tending to be a loyal follower of the lunatic; that would age anyone. Then there was the predawn flight with Helga to the United States, arranged by his American contact, a thin, lemony man who never smiled. Then there had been the years of hard work, establishing himself in America, working as a researcher for Tulsa Torrent, the world's largest lumber company. And then the many years of trying to find the legendary oil tree. And, just before this last trip to the Brazilian jungle, the word from the doctor that some of Webenhaus's burgeoning stomach had nothing to do with food. It was cancer, inoperable and deadly.

With the clock ticking inexorably toward his death, Webenhaus had worked like a madman, driving himself and everyone around him, digging deeper and deeper into the Matto Grosso. And finally he found it: the *copa-iba* tree.

His life was almost over, but he had made it worthwhile.

Webenhaus wondered how Stacy would kill him, and the thought of a dying man being murdered made him laugh aloud. For a second the grunts and moans in the next tent stopped. But only for a second. *Gott*, Webenhaus thought, they've been at it—he stopped to look at his watch—for over an hour already. He laughed again. Stacy hadn't been able to get her off. Poor Helga was still straining for release, and poor Stacy was still determinedly plugging away; both of them trying too hard and working too hard at something that was meant to be pleasurable.

There was a sound from the dark far corner of the tent.

Karl Webenhaus tilted the shade of the lantern that sat on his worktable so that it dimly lit the place the sound had come from. There was a small mosquito-netted cot there.

He crossed the room to the cot, parted the netting, and bent over the tiny figure snoring gently inside.

"Ah, *Liebchen, Liebchen*," he said softly. "What will become of you, eh? But Mama will love you enough for the two of us. And your papa, he just wants to be buried here near these trees he looked for so hard and so long."

Webenhaus hesitated for a moment, then gently kissed the child on the cheek. She stirred slightly and he pulled back. He let the netting fall shut and stood there for a moment, silently watching her.

He nodded to himself, went back to his worktable, and took up his pen.

"Dear Comrade," he wrote. "It has been many years, but once again I must ask your help. We will not ever meet again, but I must ask you to watch over little Joey. . . ."

Suddenly there was a stirring in the next tent and then the hushed hissing of an argument. Helga was telling Stacy what she thought of his alleged sexual prowess and that he was not even half the man that old, fat broken-down Herr Doktor Webenhaus was. Webenhaus nodded; he had overheard these conversations before, in other places and with other young men.

Stacy tried to respond, but nothing he said seemed adequate. Helga was right. He had not performed.

The old German heard Stacy storm out of the tent and start wandering around in the dark outside. Then Webenhaus heard his young associate start toward his tent.

He hastily scrawled the name of the lemony man he had known for many years onto an envelope, stuffed his

4

partly written letter inside, and inserted both into the packet that contained his report to the company. Then he opened his thick copy of *Modern Ideas in the Chess Opening* and began setting up the chessmen for opening variation 1066 of the Sicilian Defense.

Webenhaus's tent flap parted, and Roger Stacy stooped in through the opening. He was tall and lean with thick black eyebrows and a strong mouth. He moved with an easy grace.

"Well, you old tub, you have succeeded."

Webenhaus took his time looking up from the chessboard. The two men's eyes locked for a long moment before Webenhaus responded with just a nod of his head.

A little glint of hate flashed in Stacy's eyes. "Have you written your report to the company?" he asked.

"Of course."

"Have you signed it? With your own name?"

Webenhaus answered immediately, without hesitation. "I signed it with all our names. Yours, mine, and Helga's. We are a team."

"Good," Stacy said. "That saves me the trouble of having to write it over again under my own name." He paused. "It's a pity you're not going to live to enjoy your success."

Webenhaus looked down at the board and hesitated for several seconds before moving his black queen's bishop.

"Did you hear me, old man?" Stacy asked.

Webenhaus said nothing.

Stacy's eyes bulged slightly. "Old man," he repeated.

Webenhaus looked at him again and smiled slightly. "Yes?"

5

"Did you hear me?"

"I heard you, Herr Stacy."

"You're going to die," Stacy said.

"We will all die," Webenhaus replied softly.

"I'm going to kill you, you fat old kraut."

"I know."

"And?"

Webenhaus turned back to his chessboard. "This is a most interesting problem," he said, and castled the white pieces on the queen's side. "There seems to be no way out."

Roger Stacy clenched his fists and stepped toward the chessboard.

Webenhaus moved the black king's knight and began to whistle something almost Mozartean.

Stacy unleashed a powerful, clumsy kick that sent Webenhaus sprawling across his table, scattering the chessmen and clattering the board to the plywood floor of the tent.

"I'll be back for you, you bastard," Stacy said, pushing his way through the tent flap. Webenhaus lay on the floor, looking like an off-center stuffed owl. In the corner of the tent, the child began to stir.

The company seaplane that was to take Webenhaus's party back to civilization did not come the next day as it was supposed to. Nor the day after. Nor the day after that. It could not come for more than a week because of the rains, and then it was delayed for another week because the stream that ran by the camp was too swollen and wild for the plane to land.

When the plane finally arrived, the camp had been burned. Cartons were strewn everywhere. Wisps of smoke still drifted toward the sky. The pilot's name was

6

Jesus, and as he circled overhead he uttered, "Holy Mary, mother of God." He crossed himself twice and began to fly off.

"Down," ordered his passenger.

"There are many things in the jungle, señor, that one should not see too closely," Jesus said.

The passenger pointed an automatic at Jesus's right temple.

"Down," he repeated.

"Down it is," Jesus said. He put the plane into a steep bank, then came back around, circling twice more before dropping onto the now-tranquil waters of the stream.

The passenger was a stocky, bullet-headed man whose name, Oscar Brack, suited his disposition. He not only disliked and distrusted people, he hated them, regarding dislike and distrust as mere pissant emotions, too moderate to count for anything.

Brack also hated animals, machines, and art. The only thing he cared for in the world were trees, which was suitable since, like Stacy and Webenhaus, he was a forester for Tulsa Torrent, the biggest and richest lumber and paper-products company in the world.

The plane coasted up to the riverbank by the camp. Brack jumped off the plane's pontoon and took the line ashore. He aimed his gun in the general direction of the pilot until Jesus cut the engines and joined him on land.

It was five minutes before they found Helga Webenhaus's body. She had been staked out on top of a fire-ant hill, twenty yards into the jungle from the main camp. It was obvious that something sweet, perhaps honey, had been stuffed into her body openings and generously applied to her breasts, where it now dripped as an invitation to the ants to come and eat.

7

Brack buried what was left of her before moving on.

From a distance, he thought he saw a small stack of firewood. But that made no sense because there was already a big stack of firewood in front of what must have been Webenhaus's tent. Besides, the smaller stack was topped with a huge black ball.

Brack decided to take a closer look. Another man might have chosen not to. What from a distance seemed to be logs were actually parts of arms and legs. The black ball was Webenhaus's head, swollen to twice its normal size.

Jesus threw up. Brack came from New York City, so violence and brutality did not bother him. He buried what remained of Webenhaus, and then walked over to where the supply and laboratory tents stood. None had been broken into, and the supplies were still intact, even the liquor. He thought that was strange. If it had been Indians—and the jungle teemed with them—they certainly would have gone for the alcohol.

Outside the lab, Brack found two medium-sized wooden packing cases marked for delivery to the Tulsa Torrent headquarters. He motioned for Jesus to load them onto the plane. At first the pilot pretended not to understand him. He continued to pretend until Brack fired a warning shot at him.

From somewhere near the back of the camp, near what had been the cook's tent, a weak shout answered the gunshot. Brack walked toward it, not bothering to be cautious, and found once-elegant Roger Stacy hidden under a pile of canvas. The usually dapper young man apparently had not eaten or shaved or changed his clothing in two weeks. His cheeks and lips were sunburned and cracked, his eyes rolled madly, and he spoke in a soft croak.

8

"Indians," he whispered, looking around as if expecting them to return momentarily.

"When?" Brock asked.

"Last week." Stacy looked around, trembling and half-delirious, then struggled to take hold of himself. "They got all of them," he said.

"But not you?" Brack said.

"I hid," Stacy said. He looked at Brack with a combination of mistrust and wariness, then let himself faint.

Brack lifted Stacy to his shoulders and carried him back to the plane. All the way, he felt as if he were being watched. He dumped his burden at the edge of the river, then went back for one last look around. On the plywood floor of Webenhaus's tent, he found a scattered chess set and a manila envelope addressed to Webenhaus's superiors at Tulsa Torrent. He peeked inside. It was some sort of report, and stuffed between its pages was another, smaller envelope. He closed up the manila envelope, folded it, and put it into the pocket of his bush jacket.

He turned back to the riverbank and had gotten halfway there when he knew there was someone behind him. He took his gun from its holder and dropped to the ground in one fluid motion, a motion surprisingly quick and graceful for a man so big and bulky.

Brack looked down the barrel of the weapon at a little red-haired girl standing on the path behind him, her dress torn, her face smudged with dirt, and her thumb firmly implanted in her mouth, as if it were her only means of getting oxygen in the Brazilian jungle.

She stared at him levelly for several moments, dropped her arm to her side, then ran toward him, crying all the way.

9

CHAPTER TWO

His name was Remo and the air was cold.

But what bothered him was that he felt the cold and he shouldn't have. Feeling cold or feeling hot was simply a matter of letting your body and senses control you, instead of you controlling your body and senses.

And as the heir apparent to the House of Sinanju, Remo was closer than any other Westerner to achieving control. For more than ten years, he had studied and trained until his body was no longer just a shell that housed the man; instead, it had become the man, and the man had become his body. Ten years. Ever since that day they had put him in the electric chair and turned the juice on, then brought him back to life to be trained as the official enforcement arm of CURE. A professional assassin for a secret agency of the United States government. The Destroyer who destroyed to save the Constitution of the United States when no other method would work.

Ten years of training, and still he was cold.

His concentration was faltering. And that was bad, because when one thing went, everything was in danger of going.

He tried to put the cold out of his mind and to keep the rhythm of his movements smooth. Not that walking

11

on water was difficult. Especially when the water had gotten cold enough to freeze but had not yet crystallized into ice. It was actually easy, if your concentration didn't falter. Usually, walking on water required nothing more than synchronizing your body's movements with the crests and troughs of the waves. And all bodies of water, even those in bathtubs, had waves, no matter how slight.

Remo concentrated on moving with the energy currents as they built to a wave crest, and then just before they tumbled over into the trough he slid along to the next crest. Nothing to it. Especially with cold water. Cold water was easier because it was denser. Just about any clod with half a mind in working order could feel the energy pulses in dark, dense, cold water. It was the warm, light water that had once given him trouble.

But now he felt his shoes getting damp and that meant his concentration was wavering. Bad. Sloppy.

He sighed, even as he kept moving. It was one of those days. The dirty gray sky and the dirtier gray of the water were seeping into his dirty gray soul, but maybe it was just the dirty gray nature of his work that was getting to him. He was a killer of men. And now, because he was not what he had been years before, he had no choice. It was what he did.

He slowed down slightly to get his bearings. The heavy stench of oil refineries and coking furnaces told him that the Cuyahoga River was still a half-mile up the shore of Lake Erie to his right. He scanned the shoreline to the left until he picked out his target. He was a hundred yards offshore on Super Bowl Sunday, and no one in Cleveland was watching the water. That suited him fine because it made his job easier. He wouldn't have to eliminate any witnesses.

12

Remo began walking again with the half-loopy, half-gliding motion that walking on water requires. It took him only fifteen seconds more to get to the massive stone pier.

At the end of the pier was a large, squat wooden building with red neon beer signs in its windows. The venetian blinds were closed. This was the place.

The assignment had been in the making for weeks. The Cleveland mob was having a summit, which meant that all the local gangs—the Mafia, the Jews, the Irish, and the Lebanese—were getting together in a sort of United Nations of mobdom to work out some problems they were having. And each of the gangs in the mob had called in cousins and in-laws and brothers who operated the feudal dependencies for them: feudal dependencies called Detroit and San Diego and Buffalo and Arizona and Central Florida and Louisville and Indiana.

Word of the meeting came to CURE in the usual fashion—isolated bits of data that individually meant nothing, until some intelligence had arranged them into a pattern and a picture: The secretary to the head of a large holding company in Southern California made airline reservations for her boss to fly to Cleveland for a two-week winter vacation, then quietly tipped off the publisher of a financial insiders' newsletter; the publisher thought he was working for the CIA and passed the information along to a bland, well-mannered voice at an 800 area-code telephone number. A pimp in Las Vegas was told to send an assortment of two dozen of his prettiest boys and girls to Cleveland for a convention, and he mentioned it in passing to the cop he had on his pad; the cop informed an assistant district attorney he was reporting to; and the assistant D.A. thought

13

he was reporting to the FBI when he passed this item along to a well-mannered voice at an 800 area-code telephone number. A Cleveland distributor of fine wines received a rush order for several cases of a particularly rare, typically expensive French wine, and to get the wine quickly, he bribed a customs inspector; another customs inspector reported the bribe to an 800 area-code telephone number, thinking that the number was a direct link to the White House.

And the information all found its way into the massive secret computer banks at the Folcroft Sanitarium in Rye, New York. There, a tall, lemony man with a dry, well-mannered voice—Dr. Harold W. Smith, the public director of the sanitarium and the secret head of CURE—one morning pushed some buttons on his desktop computer console and watched the pattern emerge.

He shook his head slightly and almost allowed himself a look of satisfaction. If he was right, CURE would be able to take a major step against one of the most powerful organized-crime groupings in the country. He punched instructions into the computer for more information.

Then he sat back and waited.

The normal quitting time for most people came and went. Dr. Harold W. Smith stayed at his desk.

The normal dinner hour passed.

As he had countless thousands of times, he ordered a prune-whip yogurt with lemon topping from the sanitarium kitchen and quietly nibbled at it while he waited. Early evening turned into late night, and late night into early morning before the small amber indicator light flashed on his desk.

He raised the console from the center panel of the

desk, depressed a handful of keys, and watched as pale green letters and numbers began appearing on a dark green background. Smith studied them for a moment, then reached for the telephone.

That had been more than a week before, and at the end of the line was Remo and his assignment. Mass murder.

That was what depressed Remo. Not the killing itself. He had long since stopped thinking about the taking of a target's life in any terms other than whether or not his technique was as clean and pure as it should be. Remo was an assassin, nothing more, nothing less, the Destroyer, Shiva incarnate, and a professional.

Killing did not bother him. But having to kill did. Having to live in a place and time where so many truly deserved to die horrible deaths, where so many had well earned their terrible fates, was what depressed Remo.

And he knew with certainty that he was going to botch this assignment. He felt it inside. His rhythms were not tuned in to what he must do, and so he knew that he would do the job badly.

He was alongside the pier now, and with no apparent effort he leaped from the water's surface to the roadway that ran along the top of the structure.

There were tiny shards of ice coating his black skin-hugging T-shirt and his black chino slacks. Remo brushed the evidence of his walk from his clothing and looked around.

A hundred yards away, half a dozen men stood guard at the entrance to the pier. Though it was public property, the pier today was off limits to all but invited guests.

Remo shook his head. Guards never turned around.

Told to watch a road, they watched a road. Told to look up, they looked up. But they never turned around to check if anything was sneaking up on them from some other direction.

Remo strolled over to the low building with the red neon beer signs in the window. A small enclosed porch shielded the door from the cold and the wind. Two more guards huddled together inside the porch, trying to keep warm.

When they saw Remo, they jumped apart, and their hands reached toward their pockets, fingers curling around their guns.

"Hi, guys," Remo said with a smile.

"If you don't have a reason to be here, you're dead," one of them growled.

"Bye, guys," Remo said. Still smiling, he leaped lightly up the two steps, between the two men. Their hands, wrapped around big, heavy automatics, were out of their pockets now, but they couldn't fire without hitting each other. Each had the same brilliant idea. They raised their automatics overhead, planning to slam them down on Remo's skull. Remo immediately shot his two hands upward, catching each man in the armpit. Like twin Lake Erie versions of the Statue of Liberty, the guards' arms froze in position over their heads. Before their arms came down, Remo's did. And he buried them quickly and deeply into the guards' sternums. Their bones cracked inward, and the two men began to tumble forward. Remo caught each man and lightly pushed him back into place, so that both were leaning against the wall—but on either side of the door. They looked like a matched set of bookends, Remo thought, as he slipped inside the building and walked toward the bar.

16

The room was crowded wall to wall with people.

As he approached the bar, Remo waved to get the bartender's attention, but two oversized men blocked his way. They dwarfed him. Remo was not truly large, perhaps six feet tall, perhaps not, and lean, weighing less than 160 pounds. He had a dark, ordinarily good-looking face and dark, tranquil eyes that women found captivating. The only sign that Remo might have been more than he seemed were his wrists, which were extraordinarily thick.

Remo faced the men who blocked his way to the bar. "Excuse me," he said to the bigger of the two.

The man turned and belched in Remo's face.

Remo shook his head. "I was afraid you'd do something like that."

"What's that?" the big man asked, and belched again. The smell of bourbon and half-cooked red meat poured from his mouth.

"Never mind," Remo sighed, and touched the middle of the man's chest with his index finger. The man fell to the floor, screaming. "Help me, help me. It's my heart; it's my heart."

The second big man bent over to tend to him, and Remo moved to the bar.

"What'll you have?" the bartender asked.

"Make mine sarsaparilla, pardner," Remo drawled. When the bartender went to get it, Remo realized the man was the type to take everything literally. No sense of humor. "Never mind," he called out. "Just make it ice water."

Behind Remo, a crowd started to form around the dead man on the floor; Remo heard their ugly muttering. The second large man pointed to Remo's back, and an arm reached over and grabbed Remo by the shoulder. Then the arm dropped with a loud thump. The owner of the arm still stood, until he looked down to the floor and saw his arm lying there, then he, too, fell to the floor.

"Don't anybody else bother me while I drink my water," Remo said. "All this exercise makes me thirsty."

The bartender placed the water in front of Remo, gingerly, as if ready to bolt away as soon as glass touched countertop.

"Hold it," said Remo. "This water's not from that cesspool out there, is it?" He nodded toward the front of the building and Lake Erie.

"No, sir. Bottled water. Poland. Best there is, sir."

"Okay," Remo said. He took a sip. A woman behind him screamed. Remo stepped out of reach of another man's arm. To watch him, it did not look as if he had moved at all, but suddenly the other man was sliding along the length of the bar, knocking over drinks, and upsetting patrons as he went.

Remo finished his water to the accompaniment of eight guns being drawn and their safeties being clicked off. He asked the bartender for some matches.

"Yes, sir," the bartender said, tossing a pack of matches onto the bar.

"How do you like me so far?" Remo asked.

"Fine, sir. Fine," said the bartender.

"Well, if you like all that, you'll love what's next," Remo said.

But for all his offhand manner, Remo was not happy with himself. This should have been very simple: Walk in, get rid of them all, one by one, and then leave. But the bad walk across the lake had upset him, and now he was going to dispose of this whole building full of people at once. He knew he was going to hear about that.

Remo walked toward the door and stopped alongside some faded white linen curtains. Four men of various ages, but all the same mastodon size, charged at him, and the noise level in the room doubled.

Remo moved slightly and fluttered his left hand at two of them and they fell, forming a natural barricade in front of him and the door. Remo struck a match and set fire to two sets of curtains.

He started to blow the match out and drop it into an ashtray, then hesitated, and instead lit the ties of the two men who were still straining to reach him past the bodies of the two burly men.

While these two began to pay attention to their shirt fronts, Remo walked to the other side of the door and lit two more sets of curtains. Then he walked out the door. Outside, he stacked the bodies of the two guards against the door so it could not be forced open.

The fire was already coursing through the building.

Remo watched with a calculating eye. Every few seconds someone would try to crawl through one of the four small windows, and Remo would walk over to them, smile politely, then push a head, arm, or leg back inside.

Screams started coming from within the building as the people inside realized they were trapped. When they heard the commotion, the guards at the gate to the pier finally turned around. Four of them came running down the hundred yards or so from their posts.

A big, overweight, red-faced man with terror in his eyes was the first to reach Remo.

"Holy jumping Jesus," he said.

Remo was quiet.

"Holy jumping Jesus."

19

"You said that," Remo said, and picked him up and threw him through a window.

The second and third guards arrived, panting.

"Okay, buddy," one of them growled at Remo. "What the hell's going on here?"

Remo looked at the two of them, then back at the building.

"Looks like a fire to me," he replied.

"Don't be a wiseass," the man said.

"Okay," Remo said, then picked both of them up and threw them into the building. Then he turned to see about the remaining guards.

The fourth guard had almost caught up with his three colleagues as Remo disposed of the last of them. When he saw Remo look in his direction, he turned toward the pier and made a swan dive into the frigid waters of Lake Erie.

Remo started walking toward the street that fronted the pier. As he approached the gate, the last two guards ran off in opposite directions.

In the gloomy, chilly darkness, Remo walked up East Ninth Street, wondering why he felt so bad. It couldn't be just because there were so many people out there who deserved removal; there were always a lot of people who deserved removal. There had to be another answer, and it came to him as he neared Euclid Avenue. What disturbed him was that what he did made no difference at all. Today, sixty-three gang goons died. Tomorrow, there would be sixty-three new gang goons to take their places. Remo was just spitting into the wind, and no matter how hard he spat, the saliva didn't settle anywhere.

What he needed to pep himself up was a job that produced some provable public good, something to

20

make him feel as if he and his work were worthwhile.

By the time he reached Euclid, the streets were filled with ambulances, police cars, fire trucks, and TV camera crews. The spinning emergency lights on top of the vehicles threw swirling splashes of red light across the faces of the nearby buildings. Remo turned right and kept walking, heading for the Terminal Tower and the Rapid Transit trains to the airport.

He had almost reached Public Square when he heard hoofbeats behind him. He turned to confront two mounted policemen, their guns drawn, who were galloping toward him.

"They went thataway," Remo said.

"Stand where you are, mister," the policeman on the lead horse said, reining his steed to a stop. Nobody in Cleveland had a sense of humor.

"Why?"

"Shut up your face. Stand where you are and raise your hands."

Later, neither of the mounted patrolmen could remember exactly what had happened. One moment, the suspect was raising his hands. The next, he was standing between their horses. And the moment after that, the horses were tearing and bucking, galloping hell-bent along the lakeshore highway half a mile away.

Watching them career off didn't make Remo feel any better. So he had decided not to remove two nasty policemen. Big deal. What he needed was to do something good, really good, the kind of thing that would score him some points in heaven.

Remo crossed the street and entered the old, bronzed glass doors at the entrance to the Terminal Tower. He crossed the lobby and walked down the long, sloping pink-granite-lined ramp to the main concourse.

The concourse was a man-made granite cavern, the size of half a dozen football fields, and broken up here and there into little clumps of shops, most of which were now closed. The brightly lit center of the concourse was filled with people in evening dress and policemen.

Remo stopped at the bottom of the ramp and looked around. To his right were the stairs leading down another flight to the waiting platforms for the trains going to the airport. In front of the doors were two uniformed policemen, carefully eyeing everyone who went through. To his left were stairs leading to the trains destined for the eastern suburbs. Their entrance, too, was patrolled by a pair of cops.

Remo turned to go back up the ramp. Before he could take a step, he was stopped by the sight of two more cops at the top, checking out anyone who was trying to enter the concourse. He didn't want any policeman's blood on his hands; that would be all he needed to cap a lousy day. He turned away from the policemen and walked straight ahead, joining a crowd that was walking toward one of the darker corners of the concourse. Remo listened to the buzz of their conversation, trying to figure out what all these people in evening dress were talking about. But none of the words made sense.

" . . . cume potential. . . ."

" . . . costs per mil. . . ."

" . . . he's such a darling. . . ."

" . . . then we zoomed in on all this water sloshing around in the toilet bowl and. . . ."

" . . . we call it maize . . . I call it profit . . . units up eighteen percent. . . ."

The crowd slowed down almost to a stop, and Remo

22

moved to the front as quickly and as easily as he could. The crowd had stopped at a gateway. Beyond it, part of the concourse had been roped off and converted into a banquet hall with a long main table and a hundred smaller round tables, all covered with white tablecloths and set with china and silver. Candles glowed at each table, and eight giant television screens hung from the ceiling at strategic spots around the dining area. Strung across the middle of the room was a giant banner that read: WELCOME TO THE FIRST ANNUAL CONVENTION OF THE NATIONAL ASSOCIATION FOR THE ADVANCE-MENT OF ARTISTRY IN TELEVISION COMMERCIALS.

Remo paused at the ticket stand and looked around. There were dozens of faces he could recognize. Someone asked him for his ticket.

He jerked a thumb over his shoulder. "The fellow in the back's got them," he said. He walked past the ticket table and wandered around the room.

They were all here, all the faces that had forced themselves into his consciousness by their ubiquitous presence on America's television screens.

There was a fat woman who thought the way to kill cockroaches was to hit them with a broom. There was another one with a flat face like a tanned pancake, who shilled for margarine. There was the Neaty-Bowl man who proved toilet bowls were clean by doing the back stroke in the toilet tank.

There was a British actor who had been out of work for 40 years and had been resuscitated to hawk records.

There was a man who sold stereos at the top of his voice, proving that mental illness was no barrier to finding work.

Remo looked at them all with the shock of recognition. They were all here, the greatest assortment of pests that America had ever had, all collected in one room, acting almost like normal human beings. But tomorrow, Remo knew, they would be back at their evil work. A pleasant thought came to his mind.

And all day long he had been grousing that he never did anything good—really good—for the United States.

He found the light switches in the back of the room. Rather than try to figure them out, he pulled them all. The entire hall was plunged into darkness. There were a few screams before the master of ceremonies told everyone to sit calmly, that power would be restored in just a few minutes.

A few minutes was all Remo needed. He wended his way through the tables, seeing clearly in the darkness. Every time he found one of the more odious television pitchmen, he leaned over the person and, using his right thumb and index finger, broke his or her nose.

It would be a long time before they posed for the cameras again. God Bless America.

Remo left the banquet hall whistling.

CHAPTER THREE

Remo closed the door behind him and walked to the window, stepping carefully to avoid the frail, little yellow man in the mauve kimono, who was sitting precisely in the center of the room, where all traffic would have to detour around him.

The room was overheated and stuffy, but because he couldn't count on his body to do anything right today, Remo decided not to adjust his own internal temperature. Instead, he used his index finger to cut a three-inch circular hole in the very center of the floor-to-ceiling, wall-to-wall pane of glass. The wet, cold night air rushed into the room, and Remo gulped it down. Outside, landing and departing jumbo jets from the landing strips a hundred yards ahead seemed to be making kamikaze runs on the hotel room.

"There are two things," Chiun said. The old Oriental's voice was soft and his English precise and unaccented, but to the familiar ear, there was lurking in his speech the scream of the scold.

Remo did not answer.

Chiun sighed. "The Master of Sinanju is again talking to mud, and the mud of course does not acknowledge the Master's existence."

"All right," Remo said, filling his lungs with the cold

26

air from outdoors before turning. "So there's two things."

"Ah, the mud speaks."

"Get off my case, Chiun," said Remo. "I'm not feeling well, and I think I'll skip the lectures and the sermons tonight."

Chiun spoke as if he had not heard Remo. "There are two things. Would you like to know what they are?"

"No. Not tonight. And not tomorrow. Try me next Tuesday. I'm going to sleep."

Remo threw himself down on the sofa and fell asleep within seconds. Within a few more seconds he was awake again. Something had caused him extreme pain in his left small toe. He sat bolt-upright on the couch.

"Did you do that?" he yelled at Chiun.

"And if I did?"

"Then I will have to take drastic steps," Remo said.

Chiun laughed. He was a little man, barely five feet tall, and he had never seen a hundred pounds of body weight. A thin, scraggly beard and tufts of hair around his ears framed his parchment face. He looked every day of his eighty-odd years, and then some.

"There are two things," he said.

Remo let out a sulky sigh and lay back down, covered his head with a couch cushion, and pulled his feet out of the reach of the Master of Sinanju. He had not quite fallen asleep when he felt it. It was not quite pain, but it was not exactly pleasure. It was something like a single tickle, doubly infuriating because one knew that it couldn't stop there; more had to come. Remo waited, but nothing more came. He closed his eyes to sleep again, and he felt the single tickle again.

He sat up.

"All right," he said. "It's obvious I'm not going to get

any sleep around here until I play your silly game. What two things?"

But even as he said it, he knew it would not be that easy. He had snubbed Chiun and tried to ignore him. He would pay a price for that before Chiun told him the two things.

"Look at yourself," Chiun said. He shook his head in disgust. "Everything is wrong. You eat wrong, you breathe wrong, you move wrong, you even sleep wrong. You are a disgrace to a semi-human. You smell like burning newspaper."

"Yes, Little Father. Wrong. Disgrace. Whatever you say."

"And to think I once had high hopes for you. You, whom I trained and treated like a son, even though the Emperor Smith cheated me and did not pay me nearly what the job was worth."

"Right," said Remo. "Cheated."

"Someday I expect to find you at one of those houses with the yellow rainbows, stuffing yourself full of those things they sell in the packages made of plastic air. Yes. Beef things. And plastic potato slices. And milk jiggles."

"Right," agreed Remo. "Beef things. Plastic potatoes. Milk jiggles." He paused to consider that, then said, "Shakes."

"What?" asked Chiun.

"Shakes. They're milk shakes. You said milk jiggles. They're not milk jiggles; they're milk shakes."

Chiun snorted. "I do not care what they are called. Poison masquerades under many names."

There was a long silence, and finally Remo rose from the couch and went to stand at the window once more. He breathed deeply of the mixture of polluted lake, jet fuel, and municipal mismanagement.

"I'm sorry, Little Father, that I offend you so. It was just a very bad day."

"There are three things," Chiun said.

"You said two," Remo said.

"There are three," Chiun insisted.

"Let's get them over with so I can get some sleep."

"In my land, the young learn by listening to their elders willingly, not by being disrespectful."

"And that is why Korea occupies such a central position in the history of mankind?" Remo asked.

"Indeed."

"Indeed," Remo agreed. "What are your three things?"

"The first is my book," Chiun said.

"What book?"

"My history of Ung poetry. It is a short history, barely adequate to hint at the true beauty of Ung poetry. Only two thousand pages, but it is a start."

"I bet it is," Remo said.

"I have also added two hundred of the very best of my own Ung," Chiun said. "Would you care to hear one?" Before Remo could answer, Chiun took a deep breath and began to recite in Korean in a sing-songy squeak even higher than his usual tone. Remo's sparse Korean was enough to allow him to translate.

A snowflake
A snowflake falls
The cold air embraces it
It falls to the ground
The ground embraces it
A snowflake

The snowflake
Dirt follows
Dirt falls on the snowflake
The snowflake turns gray
Dirty gray
Then black
The snowflake melts
Oh, snowflake!
Oh, dirt!

Remo knew the poem was ended when Chiun stopped speaking. He turned to the old man, who had lowered his gaze to the floor, as if modestly declining the world's waves of adulation.

Remo clapped his hands and cheered, "Bravo. Marvelous. Now what is the second thing?"

"You liked that poem?" Chiun asked

"Great. Fantastic. The second thing?"

"I will recite another one for you," Chiun said.

"No," said Remo, "please don't."

"Why not, my son?"

"I couldn't stand it."

Chiun looked at him sharply.

Remo added quickly, "Too much beauty in one day. I couldn't take it. I can only deal with the beauty of one Ung at a time. And they have to be spaced very far apart."

Chiun nodded at this very reasonable position on Remo's part. "The second thing," he said.

"Yes?"

"Your feet are wet," Chiun said. "You look as if you have been slopping around in the water like a penguin. You have not been concentrating. You have been acting like a white man again. You are a disappointment to me. You cannot even walk on water without getting your feet wet, and then tracking up our room. You are a grave disappointment."

"Ungrateful too," Remo said. "You always tell me I'm ungrateful."

"That too," said Chiun. "I should make you practice right now, and I would, except for the third thing."

"What is this third thing?" Remo asked, as he knew he was supposed to.

"The Emperor Smith has work for us to do."

"No."

"Urgent work," Chiun said.

"No. I need a vacation. I'm tired. That's why my feet got wet. I can't concentrate anymore."

"I cannot tell your employer that," Chiun said. "If I did, he would not send the gold to Sinanju, and once again my people would have to send their babies home to the sea."

Remo turned back to the window, hoping for a mid-air collision that would counteract the dullness of the next few minutes of history lesson. He had heard it a thousand times. Sinanju was a dismal, tiny village on the coast of the barren and even more dismal West Korean Bay. It was a poor village with poor soil. Farming was bad, and fishing was even worse. In the long-ago-past, even in the best of times, its people could just barely eke a living out of the surrounding land and waters. In normal times they starved. In bad times, they drowned their babies and children in the cold waters of the bay, which was more merciful than letting them starve to death. The villagers called it *sending the children home to the sea,* but no one was fooled by the words.

Then sometime before the beginning of recorded history, the best fighting men from the village began hiring themselves out as mercenaries and assassins to whichever ruler was willing to pay their price. Because there was always a market for death and because the killers from Sinanju were scrupulous about sending their wages home to their loved ones to buy food, the children of the village were allowed to live.

The tradition of the men of Sinanju was a long one, but it was eventually replaced by another tradition. One of Sinanju's greatest fighters was Wang, and one night as he was studying the stars, he was visited by a great ring of fire from the skies. The fire had a message for him. It said simply that men did not use their minds and bodies as they should; they wasted their spirit and strength. The ring of fire taught Wang the lessons of control—and though Wang's enlightenment came in a single burst of flame, his mastery of what he had learned took a lifetime.

Through control of his own self, Wang became the ultimate weapon. He became the first Master of the House of Sinanju. It was no longer necessary for the other men of the village to fight and die. The Master of the House took that job on himself. And when it was time for him to pass on, the most worthy member of his family took his place. Chiun was the latest in the line of the House of Sinanju, and for the first time, a man who was not a Korean, a man who did not even have yellow skin, was being trained as his successor.

That man was Remo.

From the beginning, the Masters of Sinanju had hired themselves out as assassins. For uncountable centuries, they had served the rulers of every nation in every corner of the world, no matter how remote. The wages that they earned were returned to the rocky village to buy the people's daily bread. As long as there was a need for political murder—and there always had been such a need—the children of Sinanju could stay safe in the arms of their families and not be sent home to the sea.

Remo had heard it thousands of times. He watched two planes almost collide, then tuned Chiun back in.

"The people of Sinanju are a very poor people," Chiun was saying. "They have barely enough food to eat, and they count on me to fulfill our contracts so that I might be paid and that they might not starve. And so they count on you, also."

"The people of Sinanju have not starved in centuries, Little Father," said Remo patiently.

"Nevertheless," the Master of Sinanju said, raising one frail yellow finger, "you are honor-bound both to our Emperor Smith and to your people, the people of Sinanju."

"You're bullying me again," Remo said. "Just because I want to take a small vacation, you're telling me that your people will have to drown their babies."

"They are your people, too," Chiun said.

Remo was about to answer, then stopped and thought about what Chiun had said, and the more he thought, the better he felt. Perhaps it was true that what he did brought absolutely no benefit to America. For every bad guy he killed, a dozen bad guys sprang up like weeds to take his place. But there was one immutable fact: By Remo's practicing his art, the people of Sinanju were fed. They were the beneficiaries of Remo's skill and work, and if he stopped working, they would feel it. He was needed by them. It made him feel good, or at least better.

"I'll call Smith," he told Chiun, "and tell him I'll take the assignment."

"You cannot call the emperor," Chiun said.

"Why not?"

"He is sleeping in the next room. If you were not so out of sorts, you would have heard him."

Remo listened, and heard the sibilant breathing of a sleeping man. He was pleased with himself; his senses were starting to work correctly again.

"I hear it now," he told Chiun.

The old man nodded. "See. All good things come to the man who decides to do good," he said.

Five minutes later, Dr. Harold W. Smith had joined his two assassins in the living room. Smith was a slender, grayish man near sixty. As he grew older, he was starting to look more and more like the granite crags of his native New England. All those who had ever known him admitted that Smith was brilliant. After all, he had once been a law professor at Yale, and that required some brains since Yale was one of the few schools where law courses still taught law and not consumer advocacy and public relations. And those who had known him during World War II, when he had operated deep behind German lines for the OSS, never doubted his raw physical courage. Nor did anyone who knew him when he was one of the top administrators at the CIA doubt his organizational ability.

But none seemed to know the whole Smith. Those who knew of his brains knew nothing of his courage or his administrative skill. And those who knew of his courage would have been surprised to learn of his intelligence and savvy. Each knew only a piece of Smith, and each who had known him had found him dull, duller, dullest. As dull as the closely tailored three-piece gray suits with crisp white cotton shirts and striped school ties that he always wore. One personnel officer at Langley, Virginia, had once spread the word that Smith was the only man in the CIA's history to completely confound the company's brain-probers: When he was given a Rorschach test, all he was able to see were ink blots. No imagination they said.

The shrinks, as usual, were wrong. It wasn't that Smith had no imagination. What it was was that he could deal only in reality. Ink blots were ink blots and nothing more. And his integrity was so much a part of his rock-ribbed soul that he could not unbend enough to play silly psychological games and pretend that he saw something that did not exist for him. Nor, for that matter, could Smith pretend to not see something that did exist.

It was those two qualities that had led to his being chosen to head CURE.

A bright young man had just been elected president. To anyone who cared to look, it was obvious that the country was going to hell in a handbasket and that ordinary methods would not help the situation. So the new president began a massive search throughout the country for a man with the ability to see only what was really happening and with the character to act upon it. And when he found that man, he made him head of an ultra-secret organization, an organization so secret that technically it did not exist. An organization whose job it was to ferret out the secrets of all those who would destroy the country, its way of life and its Constitution, and then expose them. Only two people would know of the organization's existence: its director and the President of the United States.

At first, the organization, which was called CURE,

almost worked. CURE employed thousands upon thousands of investigators, all of whom thought they worked for someone else: the FBI, the CIA, the telephone company, the Chamber of Commerce, or Madame Lulu's Lonely Hearts Club. It had an open-ended budget of millions of dollars funneled to it through dozens of government agencies. It had the most sophisticated computer system known to man, which was able to take in, analyze, and disgorge billions of discreet bits of information. It had secret headquarters at Folcroft Sanitarium in Rye, New York.

The only thing it didn't have was success.

It was obvious that exposure of wrongdoing was not enough. Even if CURE could find some newspaper to print disclosures—and that was not all that easy—the public often shrugged its shoulders and went on its way as if nothing had happened. Trying to send wrongdoers to jail through a court system that no longer worked was hardly any more successful.

It was obvious that CURE would have to change if it were to work. It was obvious that it would need an enforcement branch. That branch would be one man: a former New Jersey policeman named Remo Williams.

Williams was a rarity among cops: honest, uncorrupted, and uncorruptible; an orphan with no family and no friends.

So CURE framed Remo for the murder of a drug dealer and railroaded him to the electric chair in the New Jersey state prison. The executioner pulled the switch, the current flowed, and Remo's body arched in agony. He woke up later at Folcroft Sanitarium, but he was officially dead, a man who no longer existed. His fingerprints were expunged from every file they had ever been in. His training was turned over to Chiun,

Master of Sinanju, hired by CURE for the sole purpose of making Remo a killing machine.

But in the training, he had made Remo something else—something more than a man; and in Chiun's mind, Remo had also become his heir. He traveled with his pupil now, just to make sure that no accident befell Remo and wasted Chiun's long investment of time.

Smith stood in the center of the room. "There are two things," he said.

"I've already heard that tonight," Remo said.

"What?"

"Never mind," Remo said. "What is it you want?"

"Have you ever heard of the copa-iba tree?" asked Smith.

"It is not a Korean tree," Chiun said.

"No," said Remo. "And I don't want to hear about it either."

"Its correct name is *Copaifera langsdorfii*," Smith went on in a helpful, hopeful tone of voice.

"I am sure it is not a Korean tree," Chiun said. "Korean trees all have beautiful names. For instance, there is the Towering Nest of Swans, The Tree That Whistles When the Wind Walks. . . ."

"I don't care what you call it or what its correct name is," Remo told Smith. "I still don't want to hear about it. I need a vacation."

"The tree grows in the rain forests of Brazil," Smith went on.

"That's nice," Remo said.

"I am not surprised it has such a barbaric name," Chiun said. "Sinanju has never made a penny from Brazil."

"It grows quite tall," Smith said. "A hundred feet or more. And it is three feet thick through the center."

37

Remo stretched out on the floor and closed his eyes.

"We have bigger trees than that in Korea," Chiun said. "Big trees with beautiful names."

"Every six months or so," Smith said, "you can put a tap in a copa-iba, just as you would with a maple tree for syrup, and what you get out is pure, extremely high-quality diesel oil. Just like the stuff that comes out of oil refineries. It's the most valuable tree in the world."

"It must be a Korean tree," Chiun said.

"So?" Remo said, half opening one eye to look at Smith.

"The copa-iba could be an important weapon in our country's energy war," the CURE director said. "It might be more important than nuclear power."

"Why tell me about it?" Remo asked.

"We have been growing a grove of copa-ibas in this country out on the West Coast for the last twenty years."

"And?"

"Now somebody is trying to destroy them," Smith said.

"And you want me to stop whoever it is."

"Yes."

"Find somebody else," Remo said. "First of all, I am not a detective. And I am not a bodyguard. I am especially not a bodyguard for a bunch of hundred-foot-tall trees. I need a vacation. Give me my vacation, and then I'll go sleep in the damn trees if you want."

"Remember the babies going home," Chiun mumbled in Korean.

"What's that?" Smith asked.

"Duty calling," Remo said, sighing. "You said there were two things. What's the second?"

"This is a matter of synchronicity, I believe it is called," Smith said.

"What is?" Remo asked.

"Beware of emperors using new words," Chiun said in Korean.

"During the war, the one in Europe," Smith said, "I had a friend. A German, in fact. A very brave man who did much to help our cause."

"That's nice," Remo said.

"For white men, the Germans are not bad," Chiun said. "Except the little one with the funny mustache. Him, nobody liked."

"Twice this man saved my life," Smith continued. "And I gave him my word that if he ever needed me or my help, all he had to do was ask."

"You want us to work for your friend?" Remo asked, opening his eyes, greatly surprised. It was not like Smith to use CURE or Remo or Chiun for any personal purpose. This flew in the face of everything Remo knew about the straightlaced New Englander.

"No," Smith said. "My friend, Karl Webenhaus died more than twenty years ago."

"How does that fit in with the copa-cabana trees?" Remo asked.

"Copa-iba. Karl was the man who discovered them just before he was killed."

"How did he die?"

"Chopped into little pieces. By Indians, I suppose."

"Indians are as bad as white men," Chiun said.

"Go on," Remo told Smith.

"Karl's wife and daughter were with him in the jungle when he died. His wife was tortured to death."

"And the daughter?"

"Josefina. She escaped," Smith said.

"And?"

"Just before Karl died, he wrote me a letter, asking me to see to the child's needs if anything should ever happen to him."

"And you have?" Remo asked.

Smith nodded. "I've sent her to schools and occasionally visited her. But we never got on really all that well together."

Remo could understand that. He could imagine what it might be like to have Smith as a guardian. On the whole, he would rather be an orphan.

"Mostly," said Smith, "she has grown up with one of her father's colleagues, a man named Brack. She's quite fond of him."

"How does this tie in to the trees?" asked Remo.

"I got a letter from her last week. That was unusual in itself; we seldom correspond."

"And?"

"She is working on the copa-iba project. Like her father, she's a dendrologist. A tree scientist."

Remo went back to the hole in the window to breathe in more of the outside air.

Smith continued. "She said in her letter that her boyfriend had also been working on the project."

"He isn't now?" Remo said.

"No. Somebody injected some kind of speed drug into a dozen rattlesnakes and left them in his car." Smith's mouth was white around the edges. "The snakes were wild," he went on. "The boy didn't know they were in his car until he got in. All the windows were rolled up. They all attacked him at once. Nobody could get to the body until the snakes had calmed down, which wasn't until a day and a half later. Then

40

they had to saw away the steering post and the door on the driver's side because the corpse was so bloated from snake venom and heat."

"Sweet," said Remo. "All this over a tree?"

"A special tree," Chiun said. "A Korean tree, the most valuable in the world."

"All right," Remo said. "I'll go. I'll do whatever you want."

"And I, too," Chiun said. "I would see this tree that the Brazilians probably stole from my poor people in Korea."

Smith chose to ignore Chiun's remark, hoping the old man would change his mind.

"There's a man named Roger Stacy," Smith continued. "He's the head of this copa-iba project. All he'll know is that you're a government man there to help safeguard the project. You don't have to tell him anything else," Smith said.

"What do I go as?" Remo asked. "A lumberjack?"

Smith shrugged. "I've arranged for you to go on the federal payroll as a tree reclamation technician."

"Sounds good," Remo said. "What's it pay?"

"And am I one of these tree whatever-it-ises?" Chiun asked.

"No," Smith said. "Actually, I had not expected you to go. I thought it would be too difficult to try to convince people that you were a government employee."

Chiun nodded at the wisdom of this. "Of course," he said, touching his long fingernails together. "I am too noble, too wise, too compassionate to be a menial." He raised a finger in triumphant decision. "But I will go, nevertheless. I will live in this forest camp. It is time for me to make my pilgrimage to nature, to renew the sense

41

of oneness between man and his world. I shall go naked and alone, with nothing but the clothes on my
back."

"I've never heard of that before," Remo said.

"It must be done every ten years," Chiun said. "But
you are not grown up enough yet to worry about it.
This will be a good chance for me to do that, and also
to keep an eye on you, and to watch out for my stolen
Korean trees."

Smith sighed. "The man to look for, Remo, is Roger
Stacy."

Chiun said, "Remo, start packing my thirteen
trunks."

CHAPTER FOUR

The years had been kind to Roger Stacy. He was tall and lean and looked a boyish, well-cared-for forty-five years old. Since that expedition to the Matto Grosso twenty years ago, he had grown and carefully tended a Van Dyke beard. His thick, curly black hair had turned white—not gray, but snow-white—at the temples and his once-soft hands, long since grown hard and strong, were tended each week with a professional manicure.

Stacy felt at home in his office. It had been five years since he had been named a senior vice-president of Tulsa Torrent and put in charge of its copa-iba project. Twice since then, he had been offered a chance to leave the tree plantation, high in the Sierra a hundred miles north–northeast of San Francisco, and return to the corporate headquarters in Oklahoma City. But each time he had turned the offer down. After all, he explained, wasn't he one of the discoverers of the copa-iba tree? And besides, he wasn't cut out for big-city life; he was just a simple country boy who felt best when he could be close to the trees he loved and the great outdoors.

The simple country boy put his $500 handcrafted leather boots up on his massive redwood desk, smoothed out his skintight Nudies cowboy pants, rolled, then unrolled, the sleeves of his L. L. Bean wool lumberjack shirt, rearranged the navy-blue virgin-wool stocking cap he was wearing, checked to make sure his colorless nail polish hadn't chipped, and said to his visitor, "So you're O'Sullivan, the man the government sent out to solve all my problems for me."

"No," said Remo.

"No?"

"I'm not O'Sullivan. I'm O'Sylvan. Remo O'Sylvan."

"Oh," Stacy said. He took his feet down off the desk, opened its center drawer, took out a piece of paper, and scanned it quickly.

"Absolutely right. You're not O'Sullivan, you're O'Sylvan."

"You had to look at a piece of paper before you believe I know my own name?" Remo asked.

Stacy smiled at him for three seconds longer than he should, then the edges of his smile broke down into a nervous tic.

"Well," he said, and paused. "Well," he said again.

Remo sat and waited.

"I suppose the Forest Service sent you out?"

"You can suppose that if you want," Remo said.

"Did they?" asked Stacy.

"Look in your desk. Maybe you'll find another piece of paper with that fact on it."

"Probably the FBI," Stacy suggested.

Remo had decided there was something about Stacy he did not like. This was no surprise. Even on the best of days, Remo admitted to himself, he could only just barely tolerate ten percent of all those other creatures who called themselves human beings. The other ninety percent he couldn't stand at all.

"Let's get on with it," Remo said.

Stacy cleared his throat. "You know about the copa-iba?"

"More than I want to," Remo said. "It gives off gasoline for sap or something."

"Diesel fuel," Stacy said. He steepled his fingers. "Then I'm sure you understand the implications."

"Sure," said Remo. "Every greedy bastard in the world from the oily Arabs to the oil companies to the coal and nuclear people want to turn your trees into a bunch of number-two pencils."

Stacy smiled. "That sums up our problems pretty well," he said. "But lately, they've taken a turn for the worse. The snakes in the car, for instance. Nothing that I can't handle if they just leave me alone, but I guess they figured you might be able to do something I can't." The tone of his voice made it very clear that he regarded this as quite a farfetched possibility.

"There are a lot of things I can do that you can't, Stacy," said Remo. "Now, if you're finished being a pouting wimp, maybe we can get down to business."

A cloud of rage darkened Stacy's face. He stood up and took a step toward Remo. The telephone saved his life.

It rang.

Stacy lifted the receiver.

"Yes," he said, "I see. How long ago? What's the status quo? I see. Okay. I'll be there right away."

He hung up the phone and looked back to Remo.

"There's been another incident," he said.

"What?"

"Two members of our scientific staff were shot at down at Alpha Camp. That's where the copa-ibas are."

"Dead?"

"No. One of them, a man named Brack, apparently had a slight flesh wound. He's at the infirmary now."

"Did they catch who did it?" asked Remo.

"No. They got away clean. I'm going up there now. You want to come?"

"Yes."

"What should I tell them you are?"

"Some kind of tree inspector," Remo said. "Look on that paper."

Stacy picked up the paper from his desk. "A tree reclamation technician," he read. "That's a laugh."

"I used to climb a lot of trees when I was a kid," Remo said.

"I don't think you could tell a tree from a telephone pole," Stacy said.

"Since when does that stop anybody from being a tree expert for the feds?" Remo asked. "Tell them my uncle was a ward leader in Jersey City. That'll explain everything."

Stacy sighed.

The Jeep station wagon was painted electric-magenta. For the past fifteen minutes it had been climbing up and down, but mostly up, the side of a heavily forested mountain. After four desultory efforts to start a conversation, Roger Stacy had given up and slouched into as much of a sulk as he could manage while he was driving. In the bucket seat next to him, Remo quietly watched the road and the woods.

The Jeep came around a cutback in the road and started to climb again.

"I'll be damned," Stacy said aloud.

Remo looked at him. Stacy was pointing toward the front of the Jeep.

47

"Up there. Up ahead. Just where the road cuts back again. On the right-hand side of the road."

Remo had already seen what Stacy was trying to point out.

"I don't see anything," he said.

"It's gone now," Stacy said. "Hold on."

He shifted the wagon into four-wheel drive and stepped on the gas. The Jeep surged forward and slewed around the cutback. Halfway up the road to the next cutback, a tiny yellow figure with wisps of white hair, dressed in a flowing green kimono, with a bedroll slung across his shoulders, was moving along in an amble that approached a run.

"I'll be damned," Stacy said again. "Do you see that? Do you see that?"

"I see it," Remo said.

Stacy tapped the gas pedal again, and the vehicle leaped forward, passing the moving figure. He yanked the wheel hard to the right and the wagon spun toward the side of the mountain. At the last moment, he slammed on the brakes and the Jeep stopped ten feet in front of the walker, blocking his path. Stacy leaped out of the driver's seat and started for him.

The old man came to a halt, smiled benevolently at Stacy, and bowed from the waist. Stacy reached out to grab the man and somehow, he later decided, he must have slipped because the next thing he knew, he was picking himself up from the frozen roadway. The old man had walked around the purple Jeep and was meandering calmly up the hill. Stacy started to run after him but took only two steps when the pain in his side and lower back brought him to a trembling stop.

"You," he half yelled and half gasped. "You."

The old man turned to face him.

"You wish to speak to me?"

"You," Stacy gulped and hobbled forward. "You."

"My name is Chiun. I am the Master of Sinanju. Stop pointing at me. It's not polite."

As he passed the Jeep, Stacy hissed to Remo, "Get out of there and let's get this guy. He probably did the shooting."

Remo shook his head. "He didn't shoot anybody."

"How do you know?" Stacy demanded.

"He doesn't shoot. He says that guns spoil the purity of the art."

"Oh," said Stacy, who had no idea what any of that meant. He was near Chiun again. "You're the master of what?" he asked.

"Sinanju," said Chiun.

"I don't care what you call yourself the master of. This is private property. You can't walk around in here. What are you doing here anyway?"

He started to grab for Chiun again, but Remo stepped in front of him.

"That's not healthy," Remo told him.

Stacy started to move around him, but found that Remo, without apparently moving, had blocked his way again. They danced a couple of steps before Stacy, his eyes swimming with the pain in his side and back, stopped moving, bent over in the road, and threw up.

When he had stopped retching, he pulled himself ramrod straight and pointed a finely cared-for finger at Chiun and said, "You. I want you out of my forest. Now. Do you understand?"

Chiun looked at Remo. "Does this one always shout like that?" he asked.

"Guess so," Remo said.

"I am glad I will be in the woods," Chiun said.

"Capture him," Stacy yelled at Remo. "Let's see what he's got in that bedroll. I'll bet we find a gun."

"No," said Remo. "You'll find a mat, a Cinzano ashtray, and a stolen pack of matches."

"Only because some ingrate refused to pack for me and to let me bring my few belongings with me," Chiun explained.

"Why a Cinzano ashtray?" Stacy asked Remo.

"He always carries a Cinzano ashtray. I don't know why," Remo said.

"Well, if you won't stop him, I will," Stacy said. "Careful, old man. I've got my black belt in karate."

"It didn't seem to do you much good before," Remo said.

"What do you mean?"

"He laid you out flat without even moving," Remo said.

"Nonsense." Stacy said. "I slipped; that was all. The footing on this road is treacherous." He looked again at Chiun and this time saw behind the benign peacefulness in the old man's eyes; there was something chilling and cold in the eyes and in the set of the face. He leaned toward Remo.

"You know this guy?" he asked.

"He said he was the Master of Sinanju," Remo said.

"What the hell is that?"

Remo whispered, "Maybe one of those California fruitcake things. You know, clapping one hand in a hot tub and finding your soul through masturbation."

"What do you think he's doing here?"

"Sitting on the mountain top and contemplating the meaning of eternity," Remo said.

Stacy nodded. "Yeah, that's probably it. He doesn't

50

look like our killer anyway. But he shouldn't be tres-passing."

"No, but who's he going to hurt?" Remo asked. Chiun turned and walked away. Stacy watched the tiny figure just turning around the mountain at the next cut-back. "I guess you're right," Stacy said. "Who could he hurt?"

Remo shrugged.

Alpha Camp was two smallish greenhouses, a motor pool, a sprinkling of one-room log cabins, and a good-sized A-frame, like the kind that Angelenos build by the hundreds anywhere their gas-guzzlers can take them to escape urban congestion for a weekend.

The moon had come out, and snow had been falling for fifteen minutes when the Jeep wagon pulled into the camp. Stacy got out first and led Remo into the A-frame.

The sloping wooden walls of the house were covered with Indian blankets. There were two bearskins on the floor and comfortable-looking stuffed chairs and sofas. In the center of the left wall was a fireplace, and oppo-site the hearth a small kitchenette. Most of the structure was open from floor to rafter beams, but in the back of the A-frame were four private closed-in rooms, two stacked on top of two.

"Wait here, O'Sullivan, while I go find Dr. Webb and Brack," said Stacy.

"O'Sylvan," Remo corrected.

Stacy seemed to ignore that, and Remo reached out and squeezed his right bicep.

"O'Sylvan," he said again.

"Yes, you're quite right," Stacy said. "O'Sylvan, not O'Sullivan."

51

"Thank you," Remo said. He released Stacy's arm. "My name means a lot to me."

Stacy walked away from Remo and knocked on the door of the bottom left-hand room. A growling answered his knock and Stacy entered the room.

While the door was opening and closing, Remo heard a sound in the air, a sound that shouldn't have been there. It was a kind of combination of a dozen jet engines and an equal number of giant fans. Even after the door closed, Remo sighted his ears in on the sound, isolating it, trying to place it. To most people, the noise would not even have been audible, but more than a decade of Chiun's training had changed that for Remo. His nervous system was no longer that of a man's; instead, it was something far more refined, and compared with an average man's the way an average man's compared with an earthworm's.

The sound must be coming from somewhere behind the A frame, outdoors. It was even more difficult to tell what was making the noise. Remo put it out of his mind and sprawled out in one of the chairs.

A few moments later, he heard the door behind him open and close. Three pairs of feet started across the room toward him. No one spoke. For an instant, Remo considered the possibility that they were planning to attack him, but he quickly rejected the idea. One set of footsteps came from a woman. Another set, a heavier walk, came from a man obviously in too much pain to even walk correctly, much less attack. The third pair—Stacy's—were different: skittish and agressive at the same time, the type that would attack only when forced to by fright.

"Mr. O'Sylvan?"

The voice was a girl's. Remo turned to face her. She

was tall, curvy, and pretty in a Norman Rockwell-tomboy sort of way. Her hair was bright, carrot-red, her eyes were blue, and her face was covered with freckles. She was wearing skintight jeans that revealed long, slender, well-muscled legs and a firm, high, rounded rear. Her breasts were large and looked firm.

Remo smiled into her eyes and she tried to smile back.

"You're Dr. Webb?" he asked.

She offered him her hand, and he shook it. Stacy hung back, like a shy, lovesick teenager.

"Call me Joey," she said, still holding on to his hand.

"I'm Remo," he said.

"That's a very unusual name," she said.

Remo smiled at her again. Smith's taste in foster daughters impressed him.

"I wouldn't know," he said. "I've had it all my life."

"Where'd your parents get it?"

"I don't know. I don't remember. They both died when I was very young."

Joey Webb caught her breath.

"That's very interesting," she said. "I was an orphan, too."

"Small world," Remo said.

Stacy cleared his throat, and Joey shook her head quickly as though suddenly startled awake.

"Oh," she said, "I'm being rude."

She turned and nodded toward a stocky, strong-looking man standing beside her. He was tenderly holding a freshly bandaged arm.

"This is Oscar. Oscar Brack," she said. "He's the man who runs the day-to-day operations of this project."

The two men nodded at each other.

"And you know Roger," Joey said.

"It's made my day," Remo said.

Stacy swallowed, and Joey Webb restrained a smile.

Remo thought quickly. He didn't know yet who was who and what was what, but he might make more sparks fly if he alienated everybody. That wound on Brack's arm didn't have to mean a thing; he could have arranged to have himself shot at to remove suspicion. And Smith himself said that he had not seen Joey Webb for many years; for whatever reason, she might be involved with trying to sabotage her own project. Since Stacy hadn't given his real identity away, he might as well take advantage of it.

Joey was talking to him. "Roger says that you're a tree reclamation technician?"

"That's right," Remo said.

"What exactly do you do?"

"Damned if I know," Remo said. "Guess I just keep my eye on you so you don't go messing up the forest."

"You guess?" Brack said. "You don't know?"

"I never got closer to a tree than a dog-leash away before I got this job," Remo said.

He could see Joey's attitude change immediately. It was obvious that this was a woman who took her trees seriously. She had folded her arms under her breasts and was staring coldly at Remo.

Remo chuckled.

"What's so funny?" she said.

"I was just thinking about what my uncle told me," Remo said.

"And what was that, O'Sylvan?" Brack asked.

"Well, you've got to remember that my uncle is a

54

pretty smart guy. He got me this job. My very first one."

"I see," Joey said, slowly drumming her long fingers on her upper arms.

"Yeah," Remo said. "My uncle, he's a ward leader back in Jersey City, and one day when I was twelve years old, he said to me, 'Remo, there's more graft to be made in trees than there is anywhere else in government. Except maybe being a cop or a judge.' That's what he told me."

Remo chuckled again.

Joey looked as if she were about to throw up and burst into tears at the same time. Coldly she turned away from Remo and hurried back to her room, slamming the door behind her.

CHAPTER FIVE

Joey Webb walked into the center of her room, her fists clenched hard at her sides. Her face turned as red as her hair, and finally she unleashed her temper by throwing a very unladylike roundhouse right at a lampshade.

Pow. She hit it solid. The lamp spun off the end table and fell unbroken, into an overstuffed chair.

She let it lie there.

"Damn," she muttered. "Damn, damn, and damn."

She jumped onto her bed and covered her head with a pillow, not moving, trying not to think.

There was a knock at the door. She ignored it; whoever it was would go away. She did not want to see anyone or talk to anyone. Not even to faithful old Oscar Brack. It had been a lousy day, preceded by a disastrous month. She didn't know what bothered her most: that someone was trying to destroy the copa-ibas or that someone had killed her fiancé, Danny.

She thought of the snake attack and with a twinge of guilt realized how lucky she was that she had decided at the last moment not to go with Danny.

He had called her from the copa-iba stand and told her that he had finally discovered who was trying to destroy the trees, and why. He would be along to pick

57

her up in a few minutes, he said. Then they were going off to warn Tulsa Torrent authorities about what he'd learned. He was afraid to use any of the telephones in the camp.

But he never arrived, and she missed him, and she was upset that this project that her father had given his life for was possibly going down the drain; the final straw was that lunatic Remo O'Sylvan.

The knock on the door was louder this time, and reluctantly she decided that whoever was there wasn't going to go away.

"Come in if you have to," she called out.

Brack and Stacy came into the room. Brack looked around, saw the upset lamp, and went over and returned it to its place on the table.

Joey got off the bed and walked to the window. Stacy sat on the edge of the bed—God, how she hated that, she thought—and Oscar sat in the chair.

"Are you all right?" Oscar asked.

Joey nodded. "I guess so. What do you want?" she asked in general, and then specifically to Stacy; "What do *you* want?"

Stacy looked nervous. "I don't know. Oscar said he wanted to talk to us after O'Sylvan left, so here I am. What's on your mind, Brack?"

Joey looked at Brack. For a moment their eyes met. She could tell from the look in his eyes that the sturdy man was in great pain from his gunshot wound.

"Oscar?" she said.

"Yeah, Brack, what is it?" Stacy demanded.

The sturdy sixty-year-old Brack glowered at the man who was officially his boss. There was no mistaking the contempt in the look; it was a look that said Stacy wasn't smart enough, tough enough, or man enough to

58

have the job he held, a job that Oscar Brack had wanted for almost ten years.

"I just want to know, Stacy, what it is you're doing around here. Danny dead, accidents to the machinery up with the copa-ibas, people shooting at us . . . what are you doing about it?"

"A lot," Stacy said.

"Such as," Brack persisted.

"Well, first of all, I don't know that I have to answer to you. Remember, Tulsa Torrent put me in charge of the show up here, not you. I'm sure if they thought you could do this job better, you'd have this job."

"I'm not interested in the goddamn job; I'm interested in us staying alive—Joey, me, and those trees."

Joey just watched the conversation. She had always refused to take sides in the fight that had been simmering between the two men for as long as she could remember.

"What are you doing about keeping us alive?" Brack demanded.

"Everything that can possibly be done," Stacy said. He had raised himself into an erect position on the edge of the bed.

There was a long, ugly silence.

"Which means you're doing nothing," Brack said.

"No, it doesn't mean I'm doing nothing. I've beefed up security all over the area; I've posted new warning signs to keep out trespassers; and I'm putting in television monitors to keep an eye on things."

"Great," Brack sneered. "We're getting shot at, and you're hanging up signs and television sets. Swell."

There was more silence before Joey spoke.

"What about this O'Sylvan, Roger?" she said. "Did you really have to inflict him on us?"

59

"It wasn't my doing," Stacy said. "The government sent him. I thought he was supposed to help us here. Instead, he turns out to be another goddamn bureaucrat."

Brack laughed. "Help us? He couldn't tell a tree from a turnip. It's all kind of typical of the way things are going here," he said.

"I can see there isn't much use talking to you about this tonight," Stacy said. He looked elaborately at his watch. "I have something important to see to tonight, so if you'll excuse me . . ."

Stacy stood up and walked toward the door. As he passed Brack, he said, "I want you in my office at eight o'clock in the morning—sharp."

"What?"

"You heard me. Eight o'clock sharp." His voice had a razor's edge in it. "Do you understand?"

Brack swallowed, then nodded.

"Oh, and one other thing," Stacy said.

"What's that?" asked Brack, not even bothering to keep the contempt out of his voice.

"I think I should have you examined by a second doctor. I want to make sure that wound's as bad as it's supposed to be. The company is tough on malingerers."

He didn't wait for a reply. As soon as he finished speaking he pulled the door shut behind him.

Brack jumped to his feet and stared at the door. "Malingerer," he said. "That bastard . . . that . . ." He started for the door.

Joey called to him softly, "Oscar."

He turned to her, but she said, "Forget it. Just forget it."

"I should have left him back there in the jungle to die," Brack said. "I should have had that pilot turn his plane around and fly right the hell out of there. I never should have landed and saved his worthless life. What did I get for it? Tell me. What did I get out of it?"

Joey laughed. "Me?" she suggested.

Brack thought for a moment, then nodded. "Right, you. Joey, you make it worthwhile."

He sank back into the chair and Joey returned to sit on the bed.

"I've been thinking," she said, "about this Remo O'Sylvan."

"Yes?"

"When I came in here, I was all steamed up that the government had just sent someone to bother us and mess up the project. But I'm beginning to think that there's nobody as dumb as this O'Sylvan wants us to think he is."

"Yeah, he is. He's that dumb. You heard him. The son of a ward leader."

"Nephew," she corrected.

"Nephew, son, it doesn't matter," Brack said.

"I don't think so," Joey Webb said. "But think about it. We both know that the oil people and the nuke people own a lot of the government, and both of them are trying to stop this project. Right?"

"Maybe," Brack said. "Probably. I wouldn't be surprised."

"Well, I wouldn't be surprised either if Mr. Remo O'Sylvan is somebody from the government, but who's really working for the oil companies or the nukes."

"Good theory," Brack said. "But how do you prove it?"

Joey looked at him, arched one eyebrow, threw out her chest, and very quickly thrust her tongue into her cheek, then removed it. "I'll find out," she said. "Don't you worry. I'll find out."

CHAPTER SIX

The mountains played tricks with the sounds, leading them up one slope and dropping them over another, bending them back and forth around crests and whipping them down valleys, and then stirring the whole thing in eddies of frosty air and sending them out into the night.

It took Remo ten minutes before he found what he was looking for, and when he did, his thin-soled black Italian loafers were still dry, even though he had traveled more than two miles over snowdrifts that were higher than his head.

In the end, it wasn't so much the sound that led him where he wanted to be, but the smell. At first he thought he was back in Times Square again or maybe on the Santa Monica Freeway, so strong was the smell of burning gasoline.

He had come tramping up a steep incline, gliding smoothly across the face of the powdery snow, hooked around a natural stone wall, and there it was: a valley, maybe a hundred yards long and twice that deep. And in the valley there was no snow, and it was not winter. Instead, grass was growing luxuriantly and a hundred trees were in full foliage.

Warming the valley, creating its artificial summer,

64

and filling the air with stench and noise were what looked like nine vastly oversized gasoline heaters, each a 15-foot-square box that burned fuel at a blue-white heat and, through connected fans and ducts, blew the warm air down into the valley.

Remo stopped to study what lay beside him, scratching his head and twisting it from side to side at the same time. Whatever it was, it looked impressive. Then he sensed something.

"You are slow," the voice beside him said. "I have been waiting here for you for hours. And your feet are wet again. I have told you about that before."

"I'm sorry I took so long, Little Father," Remo said, "and my feet are dry."

"We will not quibble over small things," Chiun said. "Did you come here to comfort me before I freeze to death while you are spending your time in comfort before a warm fire?"

"Sorry about that," said Remo. "It's your choice after all."

"Sorry. Sorry. That is all you say. Sorry you are late. Sorry your feet are wet . . ."

"They're dry," Remo said.

"Sorry. Yes. You are a very sorry person. And sorriest of all he would be who would not let the Master bring his few meager possessions so that I might not have to spend my time in these mountains like the wild deer or bear or camel."

"No camels up here," Remo said.

"What do you know of camels? Nothing. I will tell you. You know nothing of camels. As you know nothing of responsibility, and so I am forced to face the elements here alone."

"Chiun, thirteen steamer trunks just wouldn't hack it," said Remo.

"Why not?"

"You're supposed to be a wise and gentle, old religious man . . ."

"It sounds exactly like me," Chiun said.

" . . . who's up here on a spiritual retreat. Remember? You told Smith that once every ten years or so you have to commune with nature?"

"Correct. Get to the point if you have one."

"Little Father, saintly men do not take thirteen lacquered chests of Cinzano ashtrays and stolen restaurant napkins with them when they go into the mountains to meditate."

He looked at Chiun, who stood leaning against a tree, arms folded impassively, and looking down at the full blooming winter trees in the artificially warmed valley.

"Remo, there is one thing I don't understand," Chiun said, staring down at the trees.

"Yes?"

"I have tried to insulate you from the world, as much for the world's protection as for yours. So where do you learn all this nonsense?"

"What? About thirteen steamer trunks?" Remo said. "They're not filled with stolen ashtrays and napkins and matchbooks?"

"They are filled with personal treasures that do not concern you. But nowhere does it say that one cannot meditate without being miserable and cold. Maybe Chinese believe that, maybe monkey-faced Japanese; they believe anything. But how did these stupid ideas come to infect you?"

"I guess I'm a disappointment to you."

"You certainly are."

"I'll try to make it up to you."

"It's too late now," Chiun said.

They stood in silence, both looking down at the valley.

"These are those copa-iba trees, I guess," Remo said.

"They do not look like any Korean tree I ever saw," Chiun said.

"One of us has to stay here and watch them," Remo said.

"Perhaps if I had just one of my trunks, I would be able to do that," Chiun said. "But I have nothing except the clothes on my back. And besides, somebody is already watching them."

"Who? Where?"

"There is some big clod wandering around out there," Chiun said softly. He waved his hand toward the lip of the valley to their left. "I have heard him splashing around."

And then the fires went out. The roaring died. For a moment the hills were filled with the echoes of the dying flames, and then there was only the sound of the giant fans now blowing cold air onto the giant copa-ibas. Then that sound, too, died away, and the only sound left was that of the mountain wind.

Chiun and Remo stood silently for the space of seven slow heartbeats. Then Chiun raised a bony finger and pointed to the farthest left burner.

"There," he said. "Two men."

After another heartbeat, Chiun pointed to a second spot, closer to the mouth of the copa-iba valley.

"And there. The other man, the big clumsy one."

"Stay here, Little Father," Remo said. He started moving in a long, fast glide toward the two men.

67

Remo knew he was not the only one moving through the moon-clouded dark. Ahead of him, he could hear the pair of men trying to get away. And off to his left, he could hear the sound of the big man moving as quickly and quietly across the snow as he could.

In seconds, Remo had closed the distance between himself and the two men to just a few dozen yards. So, to Remo's surprise, had the big man. For a moment then, everyone but Remo stopped moving, and the mountain was as quiet as mountains ever get on cold, windy winter nights.

The light of the moon rebounded off the powdery white snow, and the edges of the valley were surprisingly bright. Remo could feel the temperature dropping, as warm air stopped rising out of the copa-iba valley. If the trees really needed a tropical climate to live, the cold would soon destroy them. Cutting off the gas-fired heating machines was their death sentence.

The big man was to Remo's left. He had stopped moving, and now he stood upright, stock-still, only a few yards from the other two men. They too stopped momentarily. Then the big man called out.

"*Allo. Allo* there," he roared in a voice loud enough and deep enough to match his six-foot-six and 250 pounds. "You will please to stop. We must talk."

The words were bellowed in a heavy French accent.

The man closest to the big man quickly slapped a rifle to his shoulder, and rapidly and surely squeezed off two rounds at the big man. But he was too late. The big man had seen the motion begin and had dived for cover behind the framework supporting one of the blowers.

The bullets cracked and whined through the frigid night air, but they missed their target. The big man

68

started to stand up again, and this time the man was waiting for him. The rifle cracked again; again the big man ducked. But this time he did not escape unharmed, because as he pulled himself back into cover—successfully avoiding the bullet once more—he hit his head against one of the platform's steel support bars. The resulting crack set the whole structure echoing and re-echoing. The big man cursed loudly, moaned softly, and fell face forward into the snow.

Remo was confused. He had assumed all three men were working together, but it was obvious now that the big man was on a different team from the other two.

The man with the rifle walked forward quickly to deliver the finishing touch of a bullet into the temple of the unconscious giant.

Without knowing who was who, Remo decided against letting him do that. He moved from behind the tree, in whose shadow he had been standing and walked lightly across the snow until he was standing between the two men, both of them with guns.

They were wearing heavy jackets, and ski masks, with cutouts around the eyes and mouth, covered their faces.

"Hi, fellas," Remo called out. Both men spun around to face him. Their rifles came up to their waists and were aimed at him.

"I'm doing a tree survey for the federal government," Remo said. "You seen any?"

"Who the hell . . . ?" said the man closest to the unconscious giant.

"I told you. I'm a surveyor. Just want to ask you a few questions."

"You're never going to hear the answers, buddy," the man said.

"That's not nice," Remo said. He was moving closer

69

to the other rifleman now. Behind him he could sense that the first rifleman had raised his weapon to his shoulder. Then Remo could feel the tension waves fill the air as he closed his finger around the trigger. Remo could feel the finger ever so gently squeezing the trigger.

Remo jumped across the two feet of ground separating him from the nearer gunman and waltzed him around like a grammar-school boy at his first dance. It took less than a heartbeat do so.

The other gunman was very good. He had lined up the shot exactly right. The only problem was that in the time between when he had started to pull the trigger and the time the bullet had reached its destination, the target had changed. The bullet never reached Remo, but buried itself instead in the right side of the other man's head.

As the dead man fell away from Remo, his finger tightened in a convulsive spasm on the trigger of his gun.

It fired with a loud crack in the cold, clear night air. As Remo watched, in growing disgust, the bullet from his gun bored a hole in the direct center of the other gunman's forehead. First Remo could see the black dot where the hot bullet had singed through the woolen ski mask; then he could see the spreading redness of blood on the woolen fabric. And then the man toppled forward into the snow.

"Goddamn," Remo said in exasperation. First he had two who could talk to him and now he had none. "Nothing ever goes right for me anymore." He walked over to the other man to touch him with a toe, just on the odd chance that he might not be all the way dead.

Behind the heater blower, he heard the big man getting to his feet and stumbling around.

He moved out from behind the machine, saw Remo, and pulled a Bowie knife from his belt, holding it in front of him in an attack position.

"Try not to pick up ze gun," he growled at Remo. "I sliver your throat before you do."

The man was a bulky, bull-like giant. Even leaning forward, he was taller than Remo, and his shoulders were as broad as a doorway. He wore a light lumberman's wool shirt, with a sweater underneath it. A knitted stocking cap perched lightly on top of his head.

"Put that thing away," Remo said, waving at the knife. "I save your life and you pull a knife on me."

"Hah," said the big man. "And another hah. I not need any squeak-pip to save me from anyzing."

"Squeak-pip?" Remo said.

"What you doing here." the big man said.

"I work here," Remo said. "Who are you?"

"I Peer LaRue. I a tree-yanker, the very best there is. And one damn good mechanic too," he said "Now you talk."

"You work up here for this company?" Remo asked.

Peer LaRue nodded.

"So do I," Remo said. "Well, not really. I work for the government. They sent me up here to study trees. I count them like."

The big man laughed. "Very funny. You one good storyteller. You have fun with Peer LaRue. Now you tell me who you are, and then we go talk to my boss-man, okay, yes?"

"No, okay, no," said Remo. "I told you, I count trees."

"You want to play games with me, we play the games," LaRue said.

"Tomorrow we'll talk," Remo said. "Look, these two guys are dead and that's annoying. I'm not feeling good. And Chiun wants his thirteen trunks. And nothing's going right, and I don't want to chit-chat. You want to talk, we'll talk tomorrow. Trust me, it'll be better that way."

He turned and started to go. Peer LaRue jumped toward him from behind. Remo took the man's knife away and threw it deep into the trunk of a big spruce about ten feet up from the ground, catching the back collar of Peer LaRue's shirt, and pinning the squirming, roaring, very angry tree-yanker to the tree.

Oscar Brack was sitting in an overstuffed chair in front of the roaring fireplace when Remo got back to the A-frame at Alpha Camp.

He looked up as Remo came in through the front door.

"Well, well, well," he said. "The tree reclamation technician. How's it going? You find any trees to reclaim?"

"Brack, I'm going to let that go this time," Remo said. "You got a guy working for you named Dock La-Rue or something like that?"

"Dock? No, Piere. Right. He's our foreman."

"Yeah. He calls himself Peer," Remo said.

"What about him?"

"Well, he's stuck to a tree up above the copa-ibas, and somebody ought to get him down before he freezes to death. And somebody cut off the gasoline engines. I don't know how long those trees can live in the cold, but I guess you want to fix them."

72

Brack was already rising from his chair.

"Joey," he called.

Joey Webb came out of her room. She was still fully dressed.

"Trouble up at the tree site," Brack said. "We better go."

They moved quickly to a coat rack on the wall and took down heavy plaid jackets.

"Thanks, O'Sylvan," Brack called back.

"My pleasure."

As Brack and Joey went to the door, Remo said, "One other thing."

Brack turned.

"Yeah?"

"There's two dead guys up there. I think Stacy ought to run an identity check on them. They're the two who turned off the heaters."

"Dead? How?"

Remo didn't feel like explaining. "A suicide pact, I think. They shot each other."

He looked at Brack, his face bland and expressionless. Brack just nodded.

"Another thing," Remo said. "If you see an old Oriental guy up there, leave him alone."

"Who is he?" asked Brack.

"Never mind," Remo said. "Just leave him alone."

CHAPTER SEVEN

At last. Alone at last. The only sound in the A-frame was the crackling of the hardwood logs in the fireplace and Remo sprawled out on a chair in front of the hearth. He needed a nap. He had not done anything particularly strenuous during the day, but accommodating the body to the extremes of outside temperature took a toll on one's endurance. His batteries needed some recharging.

He had just closed his eyes when he heard the door to the cabin open behind him and a set of light footsteps come across the room. They were too light to be Peer LaRue's or Oscar Brack's; they were even more tentative than Roger Stacy's; and they were not rhythmic enough to be Joey Webb's. And they could not have been Chiun's because if Chiun had entered the cabin, Remo would not have heard him.

He would ignore whoever it was and maybe they would take mercy on a sleeping man and go away. Whoever it was walked past him. Then Remo could hear the person turn around and look in his direction. Then he heard the person settle down into a chair alongside the fireplace, facing him.

Remo waited, but there was no further sound. Finally he opened one eye and looked up.

The man who was sitting there reminded Remo of a mouse; like a mouse close enough to his hole to be assured of safety might watch the goings-on in a busy, catless kitchen, this man was watching him intently.

A mouse. Maybe it was the way he was dressed: a polyester, double-knit, reddish-brown suit; an off-brown dress shirt; a cocoa-brown tie covered with white splotches; brown Hush Puppies. Maybe it was the watery brown eyes that looked at Remo, then darted around the room, on the lookout for God-alone-knew-what. Or the way the man sat with his cheap brown government-issue vinyl briefcase upright on his knees, holding it tightly with both hands and hunched over its top. Or maybe it was the way the little guy's nose kept twitching and moving around, always sniffing the air, managing to give the impression that he didn't quite approve of what he smelled. Maybe it was the little guy's high, squeaky voice when he saw Remo's eyes open.

He finally introduced himself. "Mr. O'Sylvan, I'm Harvey Quibble."

A mouse. Definitely a mouse. Harvey Quibble. It was even a mouse's name. "Will it wait till morning?" Remo asked.

"No, sir. It will not wait until morning. No, definitely not, sir, it will not wait till morning."

"Can I get you something?" Remo asked. "A piece of cheese?"

"No, sir," said Harvey Quibble. "I don't believe in mixing business with pleasure."

"I don't think there's much chance of our doing that," Remo said. "What's on your mind?"

"We have a dreadful problem," Quibble said. He opened his briefcase.

"Maybe you ought to tell me who you are," Remo said.

"I am from the federal job occupational survey team," Quibble said, "and we find that your agency is trying to define your occupational title in an entirely inappropriate manner."

Remo sighed, got up, and walked to the fire, where he rubbed his hands together. He wondered if Harvey Quibble would burn if thrown into the fireplace. Did mice burn? Or melt?

"Mr. Quibble, I'm very tired. Can we talk about this in the morning?"

"No. Problems should be solved as they arise," Quibble said. "Now, the Forestry Service wants to define your worker-function rating as a three-nine-eight-four seven-six, and I'm afraid we could never agree to that."

"Well, then, change it," Remo said.

"I thought I should talk to you," Quibble said. "I'm sure you'll agree, Mr. O'Sylvan, that your worker function is hardly a three, which after all is synthesizing. I mean the title of your job, to say nothing of its description, almost certainly makes it a six, which is only comparing."

"Sounds good to me," Remo said.

"And I'm sure that your 'people-function' is certainly not mentoring, which is what nine means. In fact, Mr. O'Sylvan, I would dare say that it really hardly amounts to 'taking instructions—helping,' which is an eight. I would make it a nine, perhaps, if it were only up to me, but of course, it isn't, and besides I really think an eight or maybe even a seven is more accurate."

"Fine, Mr. Quibble," Remo said. He walked back to the chair, sat down and glowered at the small man. "Anything you want."

"Good. You can trust me to do right by you. A lot of

77

people resent my work, but I have to tell you I'm really delighted by your attitude. I mean, it's important to know exactly what federal workers do. For instance, your setting-up classification—that's what that eight means, you know—it seems to me that what you're doing is really more on the order of handling, which is actually only a five. Wouldn't you agree, Mr. O'Sylvan?"

"I think you've hit it right on the head," Remo said. "I was worrying about it myself."

Harvey Quibble stood up and carefully put on his brown stocking cap, wrapped his dark brown knit scarf around his neck, closed his briefcase, and put on brown plastic mittens. "I'm so glad you feel that way, Mr. O'Sylvan. You have no notion of how nasty some people can become."

Remo was trying to close his eyes for sleep. "Anything you want," he said. Then he realized Quibble was standing in front of him. The little man had thrust out a mittened hand for him to shake. R   t   it.

"Good," Quibble said. "I'm glad you   with my assessment. I'll send the paperwork throug t Washington the first thing in the morning."

"What paperwork?" Remo asked, suddenly suspicious as he always was of anything called paperwork. He did not trust people who called paper work. Paper was paper and work was work.

"Why, the papers that will cut your salary by seventy-five percent, Mr. O'Sylvan. Just as we agreed."

Then the mousy little man was gone.

Remo just wanted to sleep where he was, but who knew what Harvey Quibble's second wave might look like.

He went to the bedrooms in the back of the A-frame and found one that looked unoccupied. He slipped off his loafers and lay on the bed. A hell of a day. Two men dead before he could get anything out of them. So tomorrow, instead of having this all wrapped up, he was starting from square zero again.

He closed his eyes. He slept.

The night sounds filled the room and Remo sampled them, first one by one, then in combinations: the howls of coyotes and the echoes of their howls; the screeches of night-hunting owls; the death shrieks of tiny, furry creatures; some cat-pawed creature stalking along the tree line; the fire crackling in the main room; snow shifting in its drifts; ice melting and water running; someone moving in the corridor outside his room and stopping at his door. It took a split second for that last sound to penetrate.

He lay still on the bed, waiting for whoever it was to make a final decision and come through the door. He did not want to kill anybody tonight; that meant having to get up later and get rid of the body.

The door creaked open, then squealed shut. There were no lights in the room, but Remo did not need them. He knew who it was.

Joey Webb carefully extended one foot in Remo's direction, set it down on the floor, and transferred her weight to it. The floorboard squeaked, and the night-walker pulled back, startled, causing the floor to squeak again.

She let out a little gasp at the noise she had made.

"Hello," Remo said casually.

"Hello," Joey replied.

There was a pause while Remo waited for her to talk.

"This is very awkward," she said.

Remo looked her up and down in the darkness. She was dressed in only a lumberjack shirt and brief silk panties. Remo noticed that her legs were remarkably long and beautiful. There was something appealing about the way she looked, nothing blatantly sexual, but a look that could make a man want to cuddle her for a long time, until she could be gently joined and then ridden like a bronco until a body-shaking explosion of passion. It was a shame, Remo thought, that sex held about as much appeal for him as did his breathing exercise. It had all become a matter of body control, mixed in equal parts with dedication to perfecting his skills.

"Then why'd you come?" he asked.

"I don't know," she said. "To talk to you, I guess. To ask what happened tonight."

Her fingers fiddled with her shirt.

"If you keep doing that, I'll never believe you," Remo said.

"Doing what?"

"Unbuttoning your shirt."

"Oh," she said. Her hand fell away from her shirt as if the garment was hot. Then she blushed, deeply and thoroughly. She rebuttoned her shirt, right up to the neck.

"Can I sit down?" she said.

"Go ahead," Remo said.

She sat on the end of the bed.

Remo waited a few seconds and when she didn't speak, he said, "Well?"

"I really botched this all up," she said.

"What *all?*"

"Finding out who you are and why you're here."

80

"You know who I am. I'm a tree inspector here to look at your trees."

"I don't think so," Joey said.

"Why not?"

"Because of that act you were putting on earlier. I don't think you're that much of a jackass."

"Just doing what comes naturally," Remo said.

"I don't think so," said Joey.

"Why not?"

"Because anyone who can leave Pierre hanging in a tree has been doing something besides hanging out in Jersey City ward clubs. I think . . ."

She stopped in mid-sentence because Remo suddenly sat upright in bed and put his hand over her mouth. For a moment, Joey's eyes filled with shock and surprise. She was certain that she had badly miscalculated this thin, dark stranger and that she was about to pay a price. Then he put his mouth next to her ear, and she felt a shiver of anticipation—one that she reluctantly admitted to herself was a pleasant shiver.

But Remo only whispered in her ear. "Be quiet," he said. "There's someone outside. Understand?"

He looked at her, and she nodded yes.

He took his hand away from her mouth and moved to the curtained window in a motion that would have made a cat look clumsy.

"I don't hear . . ."

The hand was back over her mouth.

"I told you to be quiet," he whispered in her ear again.

Joey could feel the short hairs on the back of her neck prickle, and a shiver run down her spine. Then she surprised herself and felt a warmth between her legs. My god, she thought, it's impossible. I'm not one of those neurotic bitches who fantasize rape. Then she began to tingle and shiver all over again.

"Quiet," Remo said. "Understand this time?"

It took all her concentration to ignore the feeling of warmth in the lower part of her body and to nod yes. Then he released her and moved away again. The door closed behind him.

Remo was out in the now dark and quiet main room of the lodge. He stopped at the front door and listened again. This time there was no sound. Remo opened the door and slipped outside, waited again, heard the sound he had been listening for, and moved off to the right.

Alongside the A-frame he found Chiun.

The old man was sitting on the snow, in a lotus position. With his long-fingered hands, he was scooping up snow and throwing it at the wall of the cabin.

"I thought you were going to watch the machinery," Remo said, "not throw snowballs to try to wake everybody up."

"There are so many people up there, I do not need to watch the machinery. Everybody else is. So I tried to sleep. But could I sleep? First, there was you sloshing around with your big feet. Then guns going off. Then that big bullmoose shouting with that funny accent. Then more people. Then that machinery going on and off. I could not sleep. And then I knew I was freezing to death. So I came down here so that, when I die, you can easily find my body before it is eaten by the jackals and bury me correctly."

Remo laughed.

"Go ahead and laugh. I know about you Americans, how brutal and unfeeling you are. Go ahead and laugh at this freezing-to-death old man."

"Little Father," said Remo, "in a furnace you would

not sweat, and buried in a glacier you would not shiver. Tell the truth. You missed me."

"Once I had a sore inside my mouth," Chiun said. "I had it for many months. Then one day, it healed and was gone. I tried to touch it with my tongue, but it was not there. So, if I could be said to have missed that sore in my mouth, yes, I suppose I miss you."

"Come on inside," Remo said.

"You are not much, but you are all I have," Chiun said in Korean.

"The apple rots in the shade of its own tree," Remo responded in Korean.

"*Aaaaaa-chooooo!*"

The sound came like an explosion from behind them. Remo turned to see Joey Webb standing in her bare feet, legs uncovered, in the doorway to the lodge. Remo could see the tiny white flecks already starting to form on her toes and the goosebumps rising on her inner thighs. For a fleeting moment, he wondered if it would be possible to find pleasure there, but the image of the girl's guardian—dour, sour-looking Harold W. Smith, standing over the girl—loomed in his mind like an impassable chastity belt, and the spell of her cold, smooth skin melted away.

"You'll catch cold if you keep standing there half-naked," Remo said. "Go back inside."

"I heard you talking to that man," Joey said.

"So?"

"You weren't speaking English."

"You're very perceptive," Remo said.

Chiun was on his feet and moving past the young woman into the lodge.

She said to Remo, "What language was that?"

"Chinese," Remo said.

"Korean," Chiun said from inside the lodge. "Chinese is a barbaric tongue, fit only for politicians and pig traders. It has no beauty, no style. No poet has ever been able to write anything worthwhile in it. They write thirteen-syllable poems. This is because thirteen syllables is the absolute most anyone can stand without throwing up."

The three of them were now in the main room of the lodge. Remo closed the door. Joey seemed suddenly aware of the amount of flesh she was showing, because she sat down in a chair and pulled her shirt forward, like a tent, to cover her legs. She looked from Chiun to Remo, then back again.

"You speak Korean?" she asked Remo.

Remo did not answer.

Chiun said, "No. I speak Korean. Remo grunts replies, usually wrong."

"Let's get some sleep," Remo said.

"Not until you tell me just who you are," Joey said. "You owe it to me."

"Sure. I owe it to you."

Remo turned toward Chiun, who was warming his hands in front of the fireplace.

Chiun began to unroll his fiber sleeping mat and spread it in front of the fireplace. Remo was walking toward his bedroom door. He heard the outside door swing open, then bang shut. Dear god, what now? He turned to confront six-foot-six of cold, wet, and angry-to-the-marrow lumberjack standing inside the main room.

"You," Pierre LaRue bellowed, pointing a thick, hairy index finger at Remo. "You."

"That's right," Remo said. "I'm me."

Chiun continued unrolling his mat and smoothing it out. LaRue was in his way.

Chiun brushed him aside. "Excuse me, please," he said. "I need my sleep."

LaRue looked down at the tiny figure and said, "Sure. I understand. I help you with that?"

"No, thank you," Chiun said.

LaRue started to talk to Remo again, then changed his mind, and squatted down on the floor next to Chiun.

"Tell me something, old man. Who is this person?"

"My student," Chiun said. "The burden I bear in life."

"What is he doing here?"

"It was ordered by the emperor," Chiun said. He had finished smoothing out the bedroll.

"Emperor?" LaRue scratched his head. "What emperor?"

"Emperor Smith," said Chiun.

"Who he?" LaRue asked. "What is he emperor of?"

"The United States, of course. What else would he be emperor of?" Chiun demanded.

LaRue stood up and shrugged in puzzlement.

"What's this all about, Pierre?" Joey asked.

"This man," he said, pointing to Remo, "he put me in a tree. And those two dead people, I think he do it."

Remo shook his head. "A tragic accident. They shot themselves, I told you."

"I be keeping an eye on you," Pierre LaRue told Remo, with a chilly tone in his voice. "Peer LaRue trusts you not a bit."

"Is that what you came here for?" Joey demanded. "To start a fight?"

"No. I come to tell you the trees okay. I start the heaters again. More guards up there now."

Joey stood on tiptoes and kissed the big man on the cheek. He blushed through his cold redness.

"I don't know what I'd do without you, Pierre," she said.

"Is nothing," he said. "Is less than nothing. Is another reason I come. Big trouble."

"What now?" Joey asked

"Can't anybody schedule anything in the morning?" Remo said. "All I want is some sleep."

"The Moonten Eyes are here."

"Oh," said Joey. Her voice did not conceal her disgust.

"Wait, wait, wait," Remo said. "You sound disgusted, and I don't even know what he said. What are the Moonten Eyes?"

"The Mountain High Society," Joey said. "One of those ecology groups. They're trying to close down this whole logging camp and forestry operation."

"Why?" asked Remo.

"I don't know," Joey said. "They talk about the death screams of trees when they're cut down and how that causes poverty and insanity and crime in the big cities by destroying the ozone or something like that."

Chiun had lain down on the floor. "If you three wish to talk all night, would you mind stepping outside?" he said.

"Maybe I better go take a look at these Mountain Highs," Remo said.

"Why?" said Joey. "You're just a simple treecounter or something. Remember?"

Remo ignored her.

86

"Will you take me to the Mountain Highs?" he asked Pierre.

Pierre thought for a moment. Then he said, "Sure. Peer cannot be mad long at somebody who stick him on a tree like a target. Sure. We go right now."

"Wait a minute," Joey said. "I'm coming too. I have to put on some clothes. Peer, go to the cabin next door and get Oscar. He will want to see this too."

LaRue nodded and went out.

Joey ran into her room and threw on some heavy woolen slacks. She was lacing her thermal boots when she came back into the room.

A moment later, LaRue broke through the front door again.

Chiun sighed and said, "I think I'd rather sleep in the woods than in this bus station."

LaRue said, "Big trouble. Oscar, he gone. And there is blood all over the place."

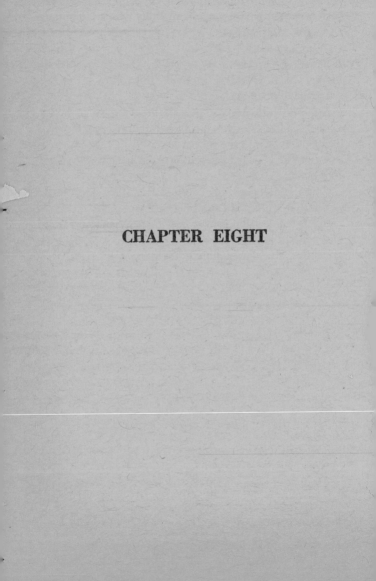

CHAPTER EIGHT

LaRue's was an overstatement, Remo thought. There wasn't blood all over the place. It was only on three of the four white-painted walls, on the bed, on one of the chairs, on the nightstand, and one large puddle on the floor. Another chair, one wall, a desk, a chest of drawers, and the ceiling were untouched.

Chiun and Remo had led Joey and LaRue back into the small log cabin. Joey took one look and ran back to the A-frame to call Stacy at the base camp.

The Master and his pupil stepped cautiously about the room, looking, careful not to disturb anything, and walking gently so as not to disturb the air currents. LaRue watched from the doorway where he had been told to stay.

"There is a tale here for the nose," Chiun said.

"Heavy drinking," Remo agreed, with a nod of his head.

Joey was back now, and she was standing next to LaRue.

"Oscar," she said, "has been drinking heavily since Danny died. He kept saying that he was responsible."

"Was he?" Remo asked.

"No," Joey said vigorously. "How could he be? But

89

he seemed to have this idea that he might have been able to stop it somehow."

"Did he know something you didn't know?" Remo asked.

"I don't know," Joey admitted. She looked again at the blood-splattered room and began to cry, long, loud sobs mixed with torrents of tears. Chiun touched her shoulder comfortingly and slowly the tears subsided.

"Thank you," she said. "I don't do that often."

Remo was looking at the bed. "Did Brack seem different in any other ways?"

Joey shook her head. "I don't think so," she said. "He always drank too much. He liked to go out and tie one on with Pierre's boys. But lately he's been drinking alone, by himself, just sitting and whistling that damn song."

"What song?"

" 'Danny Boy'."

But Remo wasn't listening. He had turned back to Chiun.

"Three men, Chiun?"

The old Oriental nodded.

Pierre LaRue asked, "How you know that?"

"The smell," Chiun said. "Different people smell different. There are three smells in here." He sniffed the air inside the room again, then looked toward Remo.

"There might have been a fourth," he said. "If so, the fourth only watched. It is a bad smell. It is like . . ." and he spoke a word in Korean.

"What is that?" Joey asked Remo.

"It means a pigsty," Remo said.

"Or a Japanese house of pleasure, which is the same thing," Chiun said.

The old man bent over the largest puddle of blood, dipped his fingertip in it, brought the finger to his nose, and sniffed deeply. He did the same thing with the stains on the rumpled bed.

"The blood on the bed is your friend's," he told Joey.

"Oh dear."

"But the big puddle is not his. It is someone else's," Chiun said.

"Again, how you know?" Pierre said.

"The man who bled on the bed, his blood stinks with alcohol. The blood on the floor stinks only with the smell of the red meat that all you white people eat. That is how I know."

Remo said, "I'm going to look outside to see if I can find anything."

He told LaRue to stay in the doorway until Remo found what he was looking for. It took him three circuits around the log cabin, each slightly wider than the one preceding it, before he caught the smell of the blood. There were two different scents: one was meaty and clean; the other was meaty and alcoholic, a mix resembling some suburban notion of gourmet cooking: Drop a hunk of frozen burger in a quart of ninety-eight-cent burgundy, and boil until the wine is a thick scum and the meat is black.

Remo came back to the cabin door and called for LaRue to join him.

"That direction," he whispered.

"Okay," LaRue roared.

"Pierre," Remo said. "Let's try this time not to sound like a runaway freight train. Try being quiet. Maybe we can sneak up on them."

"Sure thing," LaRue roared again.

Remo winced. It was almost as if the big lummox were trying to warn somebody off, he thought.

They started off across the snow at a trot, but both found it difficult going. Pierre kept slipping knee-deep through the occasional crust into drifts, and Remo had to concentrate on not just running along the top of the soft snow, but allowing himself to sink in a few inches.

The scents wafting through the unerringly air led Remo almost two miles through the woods. Then he and LaRue went downhill to an abandoned fire road and along it for several hundred yards before coming to a stop at a small cabin.

"What's this place?" Remo asked the big Frenchman.

"A supply cabin," he answered. "Peer put it up himself."

"Talk soft," Remo said. "You circle around the back."

Pierre was about to bellow okay, when he saw Remo's eyes and suddenly envisioned hanging the rest of the night in a tree. Instead, he just nodded.

Remo went in the front door. The cabin had been occupied within only the past few hours, but it was now empty.

Out back, Pierre had found tire tracks.

Remo looked at them.

"A bus," he said.

LaRue agreed. They set off along the fire road again, following the bus tracks. The snow had been plowed and the men were able to move at full speed, which meant that LaRue kept falling behind. After two miles, Remo stopped.

"What?" asked the puffing LaRue.

"Off to the side," Remo said. "I heard something."

"We go see." LaRue heard the noise for the first time himself and ran off to the side of the road.

A man lay there in a small hollow formed by the tangle of some tree roots. Or there was most of a man lying there. Someone had carved a fair-sized hunk out of his belly and he had lost much blood.

"Mon Dieu," LaRue said. "I know this man. He work for Peer. He one top-notch lumberjack."

Remo and LaRue bent over the man, whose eyes were open, staring sightlessly up at the night sky.

With a spastic burst of energy, the dying man reached up and grabbed Remo by the sleeves of his T-shirt and tried to raise himself from the ground. Blood bubbled from his mouth, choking him. Remo raised the man to a sitting position. The man strained to talk. Remo leaned over and closer to his bloody mouth. The man mumbled something and then died. Remo laid him back down.

Pierre LaRue made the sign of the cross over the body.

"He one helluva good lumberjack," he said. "What he say to you?"

"Nothing," Remo said.

"Nothing? He say something. I hear him say something. What he say?"

"Nothing that made any sense," Remo said. "Some sort of poem."

"Recite it. Maybe Peer know it. I know lots poems."

"He said, 'Trees are free. Free the trees.' "

"Moonten Eyes," LaRue said.

"The Mountain Highs?" Remo said. "Why them?"

"That is their motto," LaRue said. "They always

screaming that when they march on our land. They scream and yell 'Trees are free, free the trees,' over and over."

"And they're here," Remo said. "You told me that."

LaRue nodded.

"Where are they?" asked Remo. "How do we get to them?"

"This road. It goes up to the copa-ibas and then cuts off to the main entrance. The Moonten Eyes are there," LaRue said.

Remo was already moving off along the road at a brisk run.

"Wait for me," LaRue called. "I got score to settle with dem Moonten Eyes. This was one damn good lumberjack."

CHAPTER NINE

The Mountain High Society was prepared for anything from a border war to a briss. They had come a hundred strong in buses with a supporting network of trucks to carry their camping gear and field kitchens. In private cars came the persons of the media: some male, some female, and some none of the above.

The Mountain Highers were the first to disembus. Among them were a few left over hippies and back-to-the-earth types from the sixties and early seventies. A few more were trying to effect a working-class appearance by dressing in cast-off clothing they had found in thrift shops in Bel-Air and Pacific Palisades.

Most, though, had come for the occasion dressed in spiffy little snow outfits by Halston and St. Laurent and Anne Klein. The media was instantly recognizable; its fashions running to rumpled raincoats and ties that unwittingly advertised Burger King ketchup.

Remo wormed his way through a tangle of reporters and camerapersons and sidled up to a tall, dark man with short razor-cut hair and dark sunglasses on, despite the fact it was after midnight.

"Who's in charge here?" Remo said.

"Are you speaking to me?" the newsman asked.

"No," said Remo. "Actually, I was just checking to

see if my vocal cords still worked. Of course, I was talking to you. Who's in charge here?"

The newsman raised one hand to the corner of his dark glasses and with the pinkie of his right hand extending defiantly into the air, slid his glasses halfway down his nose so he could peer at Remo over the tops of the frames.

"Do you know who I am?" he demanded to know.

"I thought you were somebody smart enough to tell me who's in charge here, but maybe I was wrong."

"Really?" said the newsman.

"Let's try again," said Remo. "I'll ask you who's in charge, you tell me, I say thank you, and I'll walk away. Okay?"

The newsman was silent.

Remo shook his head. He touched the newsman lightly in the center of his solar plexus. The man started to hiccup then began hicking harder and harder until he fell to the ground in a shivering spasm.

Another newsman came running up.

"Hey, you," he said to Remo. "I saw all that. You can't just come in here and do things like that. You can't just mess with the press and get away with it."

"Who's in charge here?" Remo said.

The newsman looked at Remo, then down at the other newsman rolling around on the ground, holding his hiccupping stomach, and said, "Over there. Honest. Over there. I've got a cat and canary at home, and I'm all they got. Over there." He kept pointing toward the front of the bus. "It's Cicely Winston-Alright. Mrs. Cicely Winston-Alright of the San Francisco Winstons and the Dayton Alrights."

The media man was pointing at a defiantly feminine woman in her early thirties, one who looked as if she had been sculpted by a straight Michelangelo inspired by the best parts of Sophia Loren, Raquel Welch, and Joan Collins. She was dressed in a flame-colored nylon snowsuit that had obviously been designed to show off each one of her many curves. Her hair was jet black, her skin rivaled the snow for whiteness, and her eyes were as blue as an afternoon mountain sky.

She was standing in the front of the bus, waving people about as if she were a general, and as Remo walked toward her, he noticed something strange in her motions. It took him several steps to realize what it was. From two inches below her waist to four inches above her knees, her body was as stiff as if she were a wood-and-plaster mannequin. The center spot of the whole region was stiffer still. She gave him the impression of being a rusted spring, unused, unusable, but perhaps ready to unwind violently if the right rust spots were scraped away.

When he reached her, Remo looked back and saw Pierre LaRue where Remo had told him to stay: guarding the narrow pathway that led down to the road circling the copa-iba trees.

He turned back to Mrs. Winston-Alright, tapped her on the shoulder, and said, "Hello."

She turned to face him, slowly, haughtily. Her eyes met his, then locked on them. She smiled like a schoolgirl and apparently without thinking reached up to preen her hair.

"Hellooooooo," she said.

"I want to talk to you," Remo said.

"And I you," she said.

"Good," he said. "Can we do it now?"

"I'd like nothing better," she said.

"It won't take long."

"The longer the better," she said. "I've been waiting quite a while to have a good, long, meaningful intercourse with someone like you."

"Mrs. Winston-Alright," said Remo, "I think you've got me all wrong."

She laughed a deep, throaty laugh, a laugh that reminded Remo somehow of a lioness in heat.

"Oh, my dear man," she said. "You have me misconstrued. I hate to see that happen. I hate to be misconstrued, when it's so easy to be correctly strued. By intercourse, I merely meant a friendly chat. Discourse. Look it up in any dictionary. When I say I want to have a long, deep intercourse with you, all I'm saying— did anyone ever tell you what nice dark eyes you have?—is that I would appreciate a truly intimate, deep, probing conversation with you. See? There's nothing to be afraid of. I don't bite."

She laughed again. "That is, unless I'm asked to. And then, only my friends."

A dip, Remo decided. A sexually frustrated dip, working out her libido in half-assed projects with half-hooples.

"Now what can I do for you?" she asked. "Be explicit."

"I'm a federal tree inspector and . . ."

"I bet you're very good with limbs, aren't you?"

"I'm even better on trunks," Remo said.

Mrs. Winston-Alright had been closing the ground between them as they spoke. Now her body was only six inches from Remo's.

Somebody cleared his throat, and the woman turned away from Remo.

"Yes? What is it?" she demanded in the tone of an old-maid schoolteacher whose bunions hurt.

The newcomer was a small, slim, dark man with a thick, drooping mustache, curly black hair and an almost pretty face.

"Cicely, we have to talk. There's a problem."

"Isn't there always?" she asked, and turned to give Remo a quick wink.

She put her hands on her luxurious hips and stared around her at the activity. The hundred demonstrators were slowly forming up into a single-file line, some talking quietly among themselves, others beginning to chant. Gradually, all of the demonstrators joined in. At first, the chant was a relatively mild "Trees are free, free the trees," but as the volume and tempo rose, the leaders switched to another chant, harsher and more militant to the ears. "Off our land and out of our woods. Off our land and out of our woods. Tulsa Torrent's no fucking good." It was an old trick, Remo realized. When demonstrators didn't want too much television coverage of some particular action, they unveiled their signs with obscene legends and began singing obscene chants. This was usually enough to render the film and soundtrack off-limits for the evening news shows. But this was just a warmup, Remo decided. Nothing was happening yet.

He looked over at the TV men and saw them swinging their cameras around in wide circles for crowd shots. He moved around so that his back was to the lenses.

"Everything seems to be in order," Cicely Winston-Alright was telling her associate. "What's on your mind?"

He glanced sideways at Remo.

"Oh, you mean you don't want our new friend here to know what we're talking about?"

The man said nothing. She studied his face for a moment, then said, "Okay, dammit. Let's get it over with." To Remo she said, "Don't go away, please. We still have a lot of . . . talking to do."

She and the small man walked off about twenty yards from Remo and talked to each other in a low whisper. Remo focused his hearing as easily as most people could line up a gun with an open barn door. He listened in to their conversation.

"Our people won't wait," the man said.

"Ari, the hell with them. They'll just have to wait."

"They want action now," he said.

"Screw 'em."

"Cicely, my love, you and I both know what's going to happen, but they don't. And right now, they're tired of all this love and kisses crap. They want to fight these bastards."

"Everybody does," said Mrs. Winston-Alright. "But not now. The time will come."

"I don't know," said the man called Ari. "There are other people getting impatient too."

The woman hesitated and began to chew her lower lip.

"You have a suggestion?" she said.

"The candlelight march tonight," he said with a smile. "Suppose somebody were accidentally to drop a couple of burning candles by that stand of pines over there."

She gasped.

He held up a finger. "Not to worry," he said.

"All those beautiful trees gone?" she said.

"Not all of them. Just a few. Let's face it, Cicely, every war has its casualties. So a few trees die so a lot of trees can live."

The woman hesitated. "I'm not sure," she said.

The man's voice was harsh as he barked out, "Cicely, you know the plan." He paused and his voice softened. "You helped work it out. You agreed to it. We destroy enough trees so that the pigs find it too expensive to keep on killing them. Everytime they start a tree farm, we start burning until they can't start anymore. Then we've won, and all the trees are saved."

"I'm not sure," she said again.

"If you don't have the guts, well, let's just tell these people to go home and leave the trees to the butchers of Tulsa Torrent. What are we wasting everybody's time for?"

She sighed and nodded her head in surrender.

"All right," she said. "Do it for me, will you, Ari? I have some personal business I want to handle."

"Fine, Cicely," he said, and walked away toward the chanting band of demonstrators. Within a few minutes, he had them ready to go, each of the hundred carrying a lighted candle inside an old-fashioned candle carrier. He next stopped to explain to the media the route of march and where they could set up to get the best pictures. That all done, he stopped to give special instructions to six young men, out of sight and earshot of everyone else.

The demonstration began.

Remo had not waited.

He had found Pierre LaRue standing stolidly, like a stone wall, near the footpath leading down to the copaiba road. The big Frenchman had his arms folded across his chest. He smiled as Remo approached.

"Problems," Remo said.

LaRue nodded.

"These nut-cases are going to try to burn down the forest."

LaRue shrugged elaborately. "I expect something like that. You have idea, I think?"

Remo nodded. *"Oui,"* he said.

The first snowball came whistling into the band of marching, singing demonstrators as they crested the road, leading toward the main headquarters of the Tulsa Torrent forest project. The packed snow caught Ari in the middle of a chant and knocked him to the ground. Three of the marchers tumbled over him. Ari got up, brushed himself off, and looked around. Then he raised his voice and addressed his followers.

"I suppose this is somebody's idea of a joke," he roared.

No one spoke. The newsmen chuckled to each other.

"Let me tell you this," Ari yelled. "It's not funny. Knock it off."

Splat!

The next snowball hit Ari from behind and knocked him flat again. The demonstrators began to laugh, a laugh that was started in the press corps as a few disconnected titters, then swelled to a real belly laugh that everyone joined in.

Ari got up, pointing an accusing finger at 360 degrees of the compass. Slowly the crowd quieted down.

Splat!

Ari went down again. For a second, there was silence; then uproarious laughter; then *splat, splat, splat, splat*. Half a hundred times *splat*.

Snowballs flew into the crowd from every direction. The laughter stopped. The press tried to protect its expensive camera equipment. A few of the demonstrators tried to defend themselves with their own snowballs, but the only targets they found were each other.

The protest march was dissolving in a rout, and Remo, moving swiftly in a semicircular path around the roadway, could not remember having so much fun in a snowball fight since one wintry day back at the orphanage in Newark.

"That's the demonstration biz, Ari," he mumbled to himself.

He looked toward the end of the line of marchers and saw that the six men to whom Ari had given special instructions had peeled off and vanished.

Time to give Pierre LaRue help if he needed it.

Remo dropped his armful of snowballs and ran through the trees to find the big Frenchman.

LaRue needed no help. He was standing beside his bulldozer, and the dozer was parked in front of a ten-foot-by-twenty-foot, six-foot-tall snowdrift.

Remo pointed at the drift.

"You got them all?" he asked.

"Oui."

"All six of them?"

"Oui."

"Good," Remo said.

"Very good," Pierre said. "Little man, you not so bad."

"Thanks," Remo said. He went over to the huge snowdrift and shouted at it. "Don't worry. Somebody'll find you when you thaw out in the spring."

Before he joined LaRue in his walk back through the woods to Alpha Camp, Remo stopped to look at the tires on the Mountain High bus. He nodded. They matched the tread marks he had seen outside the forest

104

cabin to which he had trailed Oscar Brack and one of his attackers.

When he looked back at the demonstration, it had degenerated into a big snowball party, with the marchers seeming to take out their fury on the outnumbered and always outmanned press corps. Mrs. Cicely Winston-Alright and Ari were standing to the side, talking, out of harm's way, and the whoop of police sirens coming down the road meant that Tulsa Torrent's formal security forces would soon have the area cleared.

He would have to talk again to the Mountain Highs, Remo decided, but doing it now might just draw too much attention. It would wait till morning.

He hoped everything would wait till morning.

He wanted some sleep.

But Harvey Quibble couldn't wait till morning.

CHAPTER TEN

"I saw it," Harvey Quibble squeaked. "I saw it with my own two eyes." He wheeled toward Remo, who was lounging on one of the chairs in the A-frame. "And you're not going to get away with it. No, sirree. Not as long as my name is Harvey Quibble."

"Will you calm down?" Roger Stacy said. He was standing behind the sofa, facing Quibble. Joey Webb, Pierre LaRue, and Chiun were on the other side of the room, shaking their heads in either disbelief or disgust.

"No, I will not calm down," said Quibble.

"I think if you've got a problem with O'Sylvan here, then you ought to work it out through channels. You're both federal employees," Stacy said, "and to tell the truth, I could do without either of you. Why don't you both hop a plane to Washington and petition the Supreme Court for a hearing?"

"Good idea," said Remo. "Quibble, you go first. I'll catch up with you in a couple of days."

The little mouselike figure jumped up and down in anger. The corner of his left eye began twitching.

"You may all think it's funny," he yelled, "but that person tonight attacked a group of innocent, unarmed, totally peaceful citizens while they were exercising their legitimate rights of free speech, public assembly, and petition and redress. That's what he did."

"How'd he do that?" Stacy asked.

"He threw snowballs at them," Quibble said.

"I threw snowballs at them," Remo agreed.

"Snowballs?" said Stacy.

"From ambush. So that nobody could see him and take his picture," Quibble said. "But I saw him. I, Harvey P. Quibble. And I have to tell you that this has nothing to do with his job description. I thought I had this all worked out, with his new classification and all, but now I see I'm going to have to take sterner measures."

"Cut my pay another seventy-five percent," Remo said.

"Is that all you have to say for yourself?" Stacy asked.

Remo answered in Korean.

Quibble said, "I warned you. What this man does is un-American. He even talks un-American."

"Why don't you translate it for Mr. Quibble?" Stacy asked Remo.

"He wouldn't like it."

"I demand to know what you said," Quibble said.

"It's a Korean proverb," Remo said.

"What does it mean?" asked Quibble.

"It means that the world is filled with people who will look at duck droppings and diamonds and fill their pockets with the duck droppings."

Joey Webb giggled. Pierre LaRue guffawed.

"Well, let me tell you, Mr. Know-it-all with your smart proverbs," sputtered Quibble, "this doesn't end here. I intend to see that you never get through your probationary period with the Forestry Service."

108

"Good," said Remo. "I miss the New York City subways."

Quibble left, followed a few minutes later by Pierre LaRue. When Stacy said good night, Remo followed him outside.

"Where'd you get that Harvey Quibble?" Remo asked.

Stacy shook his head. "The main company applied for some federal research funds. As soon as they got them, they got Harvey Quibble, too, to make sure that all the federal job regulations were obeyed. The company sent him up here and told me they wouldn't mind if he got lost in a snowdrift."

"He will if he keeps getting in my way," Remo said. "No sign of Oscar Brack?"

"Nothing," said Stacy.

"The reason we broke up that demonstration tonight was because the Mountain Highs were planning to start a forest fire," Remo said.

"Oh," said Stacy thoughtfully. He rubbed his cheek, and even outdoors Remo noticed he smelled sweet.

"I thought you ought to know so you can keep your guards watching them."

"Good idea," said Stacy.

"The two dead men up at the copa-iba farm?"

"They carried no identification," Stacy said. "The police have taken prints and are trying to find something out through Washington."

"Keep on them," Remo said. "Knowing who they are could clear this up fast." He decided not to mention the dead lumberjack.

"Chances are they're just more Mountain Highs," Stacy said.

"Maybe," said Remo. "But I don't know. Guns

wouldn't seem to be their way. Forest fires and marches, yes. But not guns. Not snakes in cars. Not bloody fights with Brack, wherever he is."

"We'll see," Stacy said. "If I hear anything, I'll let you know."

Chiun had decided that as pleasant as sleeping before the fireplace was, the traffic patterns made it impossible for him to get a wink, so he confiscated the floor in Remo's bedroom.

Joey Webb sat down beside Remo on the couch out in the main room. She touched his arm, and Remo felt a pleasantly warm sensation where her hand rested, a feeling that he had not known for a while.

"What are you thinking about?" she asked.

"How much I hate women who ask me what I'm thinking about," he said.

"I deserved that," she said. "It's not much of a conversational gambit. I want to know who you are and why you're here."

"Can I sleep first?" Remo asked.

"No."

"You tell me your story, I'll tell you mine," Remo said. Maybe she would talk herself to sleep.

Joey Webb started with her earliest memory—back when she was little more than an infant and her name was Josefina Webenhaus. Of being awakened one steamy jungle night to the sound of someone screaming, of sneaking from her tent to her mother's and seeing some dark figures doing unmentionable things to her. Of finding her father lying dead and headless in his work tent. Of the endless nights of nightmares and eating dirt to try to stay alive. Of being rescued, along with Stacy, by Oscar Brack. Of an endless round of boarding

110

schools and summer camps, punctuated only infrequently by visits from the grim Dr. Smith who had been her father's friend and had taken over responsibility for her upbringing.

She told him more. Of her struggle to get into the Duke University forestry school and how once she had gotten there, her life had blossomed because of a young professor named Danny O'Farrell, whom she had loved and to whom she had given herself. Of how Oscar would visit them both at college and arranged for them to go to work for Tulsa Torrent on her father's copa-iba project.

She spoke of the project. How over the past three years she and Danny and Oscar had searched for a way to grow the Brazilian trees in all but the coldest of U.S. climates. How they were still stumped because the trees couldn't be raised from seedlings anywhere except in the semitropical coasts of the States. How everything just started to go wrong: trees rotting with fungus, equipment breaking down, key people being injured, and reports being lost. How Danny had become frustrated and suspected spies and began to snoop around.

And then he was killed. Joey told Remo how, in complete desperation, she had called Dr. Smith, her old guardian, and asked him for help, and how he said he'd try but she had never heard from him again.

She talked for a half-hour, seemingly without a breath or a pause, then stopped abruptly and said, "That's me. Now you."

Remo thought for a moment of telling her something, anything that might ease her opinion of Smith, the head of CURE and his boss, but decided against it. Smith deserved the grief he got in life.

"Let's just say that maybe somebody you know

111

knows somebody who knows somebody who might have sent somebody like me here to help."

Joey nodded. "I wouldn't be surprised. I used to get the idea that Dr. Smith was an important man."

"Slow down. I never said anything about Harold Smith," Remo said.

"And I never told you that his name was Harold," she said. "So thanks. And thank him, too."

The sound was very quiet, so soft that even as Remo sat there looking at Joey Webb, he wasn't sure he had heard it.

He had almost reached out and touched the girl, almost taken her into his arms out of a sense of personal desire rather than as a matter of duty, when he heard the call and stopped.

"What is it, Remo?"

"Someone's calling my name," he said.

She listened for a moment.

"I don't hear anything," she said. "It must be just the wind. Sometimes it plays tricks on you up here."

Remo listened again. This time the calling was louder. Still below the threshhold of hearing of non-Sinanju ears, but louder nevertheless.

"I've got to see what it it," he said, getting up from the couch.

"Don't go out there," she said.

"Why?"

"I've got a feeling," she said.

"I'll be right back," Remo said.

Outside the A-frame, the wind swirled the sound around, through the air, until it seemed to Remo as if it came from everywhere and nowhere.

He started off, over the snow, putting twenty-five

112

yards of distance between himself and the cabin. Then he stopped to listen. The sound was softer than it had been. Wrong direction.

He tried moving toward the right side of the A-frame. Same result.

It was only when he got behind the cabin and took a position twenty-five yards behind it that the swirling, eerie sound seemed to grow a little louder.

"Remo," it hissed. "Remo. Remo. Remo." Over and over, like the soundtrack from a nightmare of horror and death.

He knew the direction the sound came from now, but the gusting, whistling winds still made it difficult to pin down the source.

It was slow work. Five yards forward. Was the sound louder? No? Then back five yards, and move off five yards in another direction. Slowly, he saw that the sound was taking him farther and farther from the A-frame. And still the same single name being called out, over and over: "Remo. Remo. Remo." He was getting close now, close enough to know that the voice was the practiced, whispering hiss of someone, probably a man, trying not to let his voice be recognized.

He looked through the darkness of the night but saw no one. He heard no movement, no unusual sound except his name, muffled, being called again and again.

It was getting much louder now. He knew he should be almost on top of the caller. But still he saw nothing. The sound seemed almost to come from below his feet.

He looked down but before he could inspect the snow he stood on, there was another sound, a strong whooshing sound. He looked up, back across the hundred yards, toward the back of the A-frame.

113

In horror, he saw flames burst from the rear windows of the A-frame. He started to run, but he had taken only three steps when the cabin lodge exploded before his eyes.

And Joey and Chiun were inside.

CHAPTER ELEVEN

The air was filled with flying, flaming bits of wood. They peppered Remo's face and body as he ran across the snow back toward the A-frame. Both sloping side walls had been blown open. Flames poured up through the opening where the peak of the building had been. The soft smell of pine that permeated the night air had surrendered to the pungent aroma of burning wood.

As Remo neared the building, he could see that even the interior walls that had marked the bedrooms had been blown out. As he reached the back wall of the building, he dove without hesitation through a blown-out opening in the wood, spun, and landed on his feet inside what was left of the A-frame.

Joey's bedroom had been to his right. The walls were gone and he could see only her bed. The bedding was aflame, and fire licked from around Remo's feet up around his face. But there was no darkened lump of body lying in the bed. He ran into that area, keeping flames away from his face with the movements of his arms in front of his body, and carefully looked around the flaming wreckage of the bed for her body. But there was no body, not alongside the bed or under the bed, or anywhere on the floor.

He ran to the other side of the A-frame, where his

116

bedroom had been and where Chiun had been sleeping on the floor. The bed there too was aflame.

But no Chiun. No sign of the old man's body. Remo could not even find a trace of the fiber sleeping mat that the old man had carefully unrolled on the floor.

His stomach sank. The blast might have been so powerful that their bodies were literally blown out of the building.

He heard a creaking sound and looked up just as another section of the splintered side wall broke loose and crashed down toward him. Remo dodged the wall, took one last look around, then bolted for the front of the building, where the framing for the original front door still stood, the door long since blown away, but the framing standing as if it were an invitation to safety. As he ran, more and more of the sloping walls broke loose and peppered him with flame. The floor was burning also, and he could feel the heat of it under his shoes.

He burst through the opening of the building out into the clearing in front of the A-frame. He breathed deep to rid his lungs of smoke. And then he stopped.

Sitting under a tree, his legs folded tightly, his hands clasped in his lap in repose, was Chiun. Standing alongside him, both of them looking at the fire and at Remo, was Joey Webb.

Chiun looked up at the woman, nodded toward Remo, and said *"Now* he comes."

Remo smiled as he jogged toward them. "You're all right," he said.

"No thanks to you," Chiun said.

"What happened?" Remo asked.

"My sleep was interrupted," Chiun said.

"Besides that," asked Remo.

"I was sleeping," Chiun said, "thinking that I was

117

safe with you on guard. I heard a noise. I paid it no mind. My prize student was standing guard in the night, and all was safe. So I thought."

"What happened, Chiun?" Remo asked again. "Save the carping for some other time."

"Carping? Is it carping when I relate to you how this child and I almost died?" He looked up at Joey. "Is that carping?"

She shrugged her shoulders.

"See," Chiun told Remo. "It is not carping."

"All right, get on with it," Remo said. "I give up."

"Where was I?" Chiun asked.

"You heard a noise. You thought I was on guard. Little did you know that I was down at the neighborhood saloon having a double Scotch on the rocks with a twist."

"Right," said Chiun evenly. "I heard a noise. I paid it no mind. Then I smelled fumes. The fumes of gasoline. Still I paid no mind. I knew you would protect us. So I slept on."

"And?"

"And then I heard the whoosh of flames. I jumped to my feet. I knew there was not a second to waste if I was to save my abandoned, unguarded body from disaster. I found this child in the next room. At great danger to my own life, I grabbed her up and we fled through the front door of the building just before it exploded. A boom."

"Bomb," Remo said. "Somebody set a bomb."

"Obviously," Chiun said. "It was the closest escape of my life. A moment's hesitation would have doomed us both. Fortunately, Remo, I never trusted you, so I was on my guard, ready to meet disaster if it came."

118

Remo looked down at the snow next to Chiun. He pointed to the object there.

"Chiun," he said.

"Yes, ingrate," Chiun said.

"If this was all so nip and tuck and a split-second dash to safety, and all that . . ."

"It was," said Chiun. "It was just like that."

"If it was," Remo said, "how'd you have time to roll up your sleeping mat and take it with you?"

Chiun looked at Remo, at the sleeping mat, then back at Remo again.

"Do you know what sleeping mats cost these days?" he said.

"No sign of who triggered the place?" Remo asked.

Chiun shook his head. "There were two of them. I could hear them bumping around like bison, whispering to each other, splashing things from cans. And then there was that friend of yours, screaming your name in the night."

Remo was puzzled for a second, until he realized Chiun was referring to the whispering voice that had gently called his name. He focused his ears for a moment, but the sound was drowned out by the crackling of flames.

"And that thunkety-thunk of all that machinery keeping those trees warm," Chiun groused. "It is impossible to sleep up here."

"But you didn't see who set the fire," Remo said.

"No. You expect me to do everything for you?"

They looked up as Pierre LaRue charged into the clearing.

His face was anguished, but when he saw Joey standing safely next to Remo and Chiun, the tension went

119

from his countenance. He smiled as he came up and tossed a heavy woolen blanket around her shoulders.

"Peer was plenty worried, you bet," he said. "What happened here?" he asked Remo.

"A bomb," Remo said. "We don't know who."

"Damn Moonten Eyes," said Peer, with a deep, throaty growl. "They got to be doing this thing."

"Maybe you're right," Remo said. "Maybe you're right."

From down the road, they heard the whoop of the fire engine belonging to Tulsa Torrent, and as it pulled into the clearing, Remo saw Roger Stacy sitting on the front seat next to the driver.

When Stacy saw the burning building reduced to rubble, he shook his head to the driver. There was no point in pouring water on a building already destroyed.

"Just back off," he said. "Make sure nothing spreads to the trees."

He hopped down from the cab of the fire truck, and the truck pulled away, back onto the road to a point where it commanded a view of both the front and back of the building.

Stacy joined the four other people in front of the building.

"Sabotage?" he asked Remo.

Remo nodded. "Gasoline and a bomb."

"Thank God nobody was hurt."

The crackling sound of the fire was dying as the A-frame was slowly burning itself into ash. Remo could again hear the wind whistling overhead, and then he heard another sound.

He looked down toward Chiun. The old man had

120

heard it, too. He nodded over his left shoulder, indicating that it came from that direction.

Without a word, Remo ran off toward the edge of the clearing. Just inside the wall of trees, he found the source of the sound.

Oscar Brack had been burned to the color of raw steak. His face was blistered, and all the hair had been singed from his face. His clothing was charred, and his lips were cracked, raw flesh showing through the broken skin.

He was sitting against the base of a tree, his hands folded over his stomach, where blood still oozed from a ripped-open wound.

He was trying to whistle, but his burned lips made no more than a hiss. Over and over again, he tried to whistle. Remo recognized the tune: the opening bars of "Danny Boy."

He knelt next to the man. Could it have been Brack who started the fire and explosion at the A-frame? It made no sense. Brack was almost like a father to Joey. What would have driven him to try to kill her? And yet, here he was, and the burns that covered his body were evidence of his involvement.

"Brack, what happened?" Remo said.

He moved the man's hands aside to look at the stomach wound. He could see raw innards, and he shook his head and refolded the man's hands.

The stench of alcohol poured from Brack's body.

"Joey," he hissed. "No good. He was no good. Not for her. A traitor." Then he lapsed into a temporary trance, staring straight ahead, trying to whistle again.

Remo sensed Chiun standing next to him.

He looked up at the old man.

"No hope, Little Father?" he asked.

Chiun shook his head.

The whistling stopped, and Brack began to whimper like a hurt child. Chiun knelt on the other side of the man and, with his fingers, pressed into different spots on the big man's body, deadening nerve endings that had been damaged by his injuries and his burns into never-ending sources of pain, pulsating pain.

Brack leaned his head back and took a big sip of air. "Traitor, traitor," he said. Then he slumped forward again.

Chiun kept working his body with his fingers. The man's head lifted again and his eyes opened. He looked toward Remo, than at Chiun.

"I don't know what that is, old man," he groaned. "But don't stop."

"You're going to be all right," Remo said.

"No, I'm not. I'm dying. Brack dying."

"What happened here?" Remo said. "Did you start the fire?"

Brack shook his head, angrily, from side to side, even though it was apparent that each movement caused him more pain.

"No. Trying to save Joey. Always try to save Joey." He paused and seemed to drift. "Joey," he called softly. "He was a traitor. No good for us."

"Who was a traitor?" Remo said.

"Danny. Danny a traitor."

Remo thought for a moment before he remembered that Danny had been Joey Webb's fiancé, the man killed in the carful of crazed snakes.

"Danny took money to betray project. To kill copaibas," Brack said.

"From who?" Remo asked.

Brack shook his head. "The Association. Then he

was worried . . . somebody found out . . . he was going to quit . . . then they killed him."

"Who killed him?" Remo pressed. He looked at Chiun. The old man was shaking his head. Brack had little time left.

"They came tonight," Brack said. "To talk. They knew I found out. Got me with knife. I got them too. Ran away to cabin. They found me there. Thought I was dead. Heard them talk about blowing up cabin. Came back for Joey."

"There was another man killed. A lumberjack," Remo said. "Was he one of them?"

"No," Brack grunted painfully. "He stumbled in. They killed him. I tried . . . get back . . . save Joey."

Remo shook his head. He could see the wounded Oscar Brack dragging his injured broken body for miles through the snow trying to warn Joey Webb. He must have reached the A-frame just too late, just as it exploded, and he was blown back into this stand of trees.

Remo watched as Chiun touched Brack in places that should have helped him, that could have kept him alive. But the old man had no desire to live.

"Who were the men?" Remo asked. "Who were the men from the Association?"

Brack smiled a smile that was much too wide. His upper gums showed; they had turned blue. He whistled a breezy version of "Danny Boy," then began to gasp.

Remo reached out to him. It was too late.

When Remo stood up, he saw Roger Stacy and Pierre LaRue standing behind him. They had been watching, listening.

"Any of that make any sense to you?" Remo asked them. Both men just shook their heads.

Chiun and Remo walked back to the clearing where Joey Webb leaned against a tree, watching her A-frame headquarters settle down into smoldering embers and ash.

As they walked, Chiun said, "This is very bad."

"It really is," Remo agreed.

"Then why don't you do something about it?"

Something in Chiun's voice made Remo ask, "What are you talking about?"

"That friend of yours who has been yelling your name all night. Now he is whistling."

Remo did not understand at first. Then he listened. In the growingly silent night there was a faint whistle from behind where the A-frame had stood—from the area where someone had been calling his name earlier.

Remo nodded and ran past the building, across the hundred yards of snow. He found the spot where he had been standing, where the sound had seemed the loudest. Now there was only a faint whistle coming from below his feet somewhere.

Remo reached down into a snowdrift and found it— a battery-operated cassette tape player, whistling now with the signal that it had reached the end of the tape.

Remo pressed a button on the wet machine to run the tape back a few feet. Then he pressed the play button and the hissing, whispering voice sounded over again.

"Remo . . . Remo . . . Remo . . ."

He turned off the machine angrily. Someone had planted this out here to get Remo out of the A-frame, so that it could be blown up without his interference, and an anger overwhelmed him that he had been used as a pawn, a dupe by someone.

Whoever that someone was would pay.

CHAPTER TWELVE

There was nothing left in the A-frame to salvage, so Pierre LaRue had brought in a bulldozer to level the wreckage of the building and then bury it in snow.

Roger Stacy had told Joey to move into Oscar Brack's log cabin and had helped wipe it clean of its more odious bloodstains.

Remo told Stacy to double his guard on the copa-iba tree farm. "Make sure they have guns and make sure they know how to use them," Remo said. "Tell them to shoot anything that moves."

Stacy nodded. "What are you going to do?"

"I'm going to sleep," Remo said.

Finally, he and Chiun and Joey were in the log cabin. LaRue had left after burying the A-frame next door. Stacy had gone back to the main camp.

Joey had built a good, roaring fire. Chiun's sleeping mat was unrolled on the floor in a corner, and he was sleeping.

Joey and Remo sat in front of the fire.

"Poor Oscar," she said.

"He was trying to save your life."

"... many deaths," she said.

"... dded.

"... to come," he said coldly. "More to ...ressed the buttons on the tape recor-
...he snow.

126

CHAPTER THIRTEEN

It was afternoon. Remo had spent much of the day wandering through the woods where they had found Oscar Brack, where he had found the buried tape recorder, looking for something, anything, that would indicate who was behind the violence.

But he found nothing.

Who was behind the violence? He didn't know. And if the trees were the target, why not just have burned them down? Why kill? Why kill Danny O'Farrell, Joey's fiancé? Why kill Oscar Brack? Why try to kill Joey Webb?

Maybe the trees could be replaced too easily for burning them down to mean anything. But perhaps the brains at work trying to make the copa-ibas an alternate source of oil for America, perhaps those brains were not easily replaceable. Maybe that was the reason for the murders and the attempts on Joey.

But who? Who had used the tape recorder to lure him from the A-frame last night before putting it to the torch?

Who had killed Danny O'Farrell and Brack?

Last night, when the A-frame went ablaze, Pierre LaRue had said instantly that it was the work of the Mountain Highs. After all they *had* tried to set the forest ablaze earlier in the night. But, Remo felt, somehow killing would not be their style. And who was to say that it wasn't LaRue or Roger Stacy who were behind the killings?

So many questions and so few answers.

Remo walked back to Alpha Camp. He decided he had to start somewhere, and the Mountain Highs were as good a place as anywhere else.

He reached the log cabin just as Joey and Chiun were stepping outside.

"We're going to look at the copa-ibas," she said. "Chiun has an idea."

Remo leaned close and whispered, "He has an idea that this is a Korean tree that you people stole from his country. Be careful."

Joey just nodded and smiled. "There was a phone call for you," she said.

"Who?"

"No message. But it sounded like . . . well, like Dr. Smith."

"Thanks," Remo said. "Do you know where the Mountain Highs camp out?"

Joey pointed to the direction of the main road and told him he could find their camp about three miles from the main office of Tulsa Torrent.

"You going there?" she said.

"Maybe," said Remo. "Have to start looking somewhere."

"Be careful," she said.

"I'm always careful."

It wasn't really a town. It was just a small widening in the road as it passed through the California hills, and there was a gas station and a small grocery store. Behind these roadside structures a few hundred yards down the road, Remo could see the tents that belonged to the Mountain High Society.

He stopped in at the grocery store and dialed Smith's 800 area-code number.

Smith picked up the telephone in his darkened office at Folcroft Sanitarium.

"You called?" Remo said.

"Have you found out anything?"

"Nothing yet," Remo said.

"I heard of the trouble last night."

"Yeah," Remo said. "We've had nothing but trouble. Joey's all right, though."

"She is no more important than anyone else involved in this matter," Smith said sternly. "Do not let personal considerations . . ."

"You're a cold-assed fish," Remo said. "You helped raise the kid."

"I know," Smith said.

There was an awkward pause and Remo said, "Have you found out who those two guys were who tried to burn down the copa-ibas last night?"

"No," Smith said. "No information has been received yet in Washington."

"Damn local police," Remo said. "They were supposed to get the prints out right away, to try to identify them."

"I will keep my eyes open," Smith said. "Anything else?"

"Yes," Remo said. "A tape recorder. You think you could trace it from a serial number?"

"Perhaps. What is the number?"

Remo read him a long nine-digit number, written on the back of a matchbook.

"Whoever owns that recorder is involved," Remo said.

"I will try to run it down," Smith said. "Anything else you need?"

"You might run the Mountain High Society through your computers. I don't know if they're involved or not, but they're certainly all over this joint."

"Fine," Smith said. "I'll check."

"Oh, and one last thing," Remo said.

"What is that?"

"Smile. Remember this is the first day of the rest of your life."

"I'll keep that in mind," Smith said as he hung up.

For a gang of a hundred, the Mountain Highs had a small encampment, Remo thought as he approached it on foot.

There was a large trailer home set in back of the clearing. Scattered around the grounds in front of it were a half-dozen high-walled tents, which could sleep no more than four each.

Remo remembered all the designer jeans and snow-suits he had seen last night at the protest rally and decided that the majority of the Mountain Highs had chosen to forego the wilderness and sleep in hotel rooms in the nearby town. But he was interested in only one of them.

He found her sitting in the trailer, on a sofa, drinking a martini with olives. Music played from a large wall-hung stereo. Through the back windows of the trailer, the sun was turning orange as it moved down toward the horizon.

She looked up as Remo came through the front door

131

without bothering to knock. When she saw who it was, she smiled.

"I was expecting you," she said.

"I know," said Remo. He watched as Cicely Winston-Alright stood and stretched herself. She was wearing a tight T-shirt and skin-tight slacks.

She showed him a lot of teeth in a milk-white face. "Can I give you something? Anything?"

"Everything," Remo said and waited for her to put down her martini glass, before lifting her in his arms and carrying her over to the waiting bed.

There were thirty-seven steps in bringing a woman to total sexual ecstasy, and Remo had learned them many years before, back when he had been normal and sex had been a pleasure and not just another technique to learn perfectly or face Chiun's wrath.

But only once before had Remo ever found a woman who could manage to outlast step thirteen, even though Chiun regularly insisted that all Korean women progressed through each of the preliminary thirty-six steps before enjoying—if that was a strong enough word— the mind-numbing, soul-shattering release of the final, thirty-seventh step. Remo had seen women of Chiun's village, though, and he suspected that carrying off the thirty-seven steps might be the only way for a man to stay awake during the act.

But Cicely Winston-Alright was something else. Remo was up to step twenty-two. He had thought he could break down the woman's reserve, that knot of hardness that kept her mid-section stiff and unyielding, but he might as well have been making love to a log.

He moved to step twenty-three. Cicely smiled at him. Step twenty-four, and she allowed that it was nice.

132

It was only at step twenty-seven when she began to react. She started moaning, alternating short, biting screams with the tearful crying of his name and insistent demands for more.

Remo gave her more. He had gotten her halfway through step twenty-eight when she gulped two large drafts of air and tensed her body.

It was the right time, Remo decided. He smiled and lowered his face to her ear. "Who's doing the killings at the Tulsa Torrent camp?"

"Oh, Remo, darling," she said softly. "You're a wonderful lover. Really wonderful."

"Thanks," he said. She shouldn't have been able to do that. She should have been putty in his hands, ready to answer anything he asked.

Step twenty-nine. Another smile, another approach toward her ear, another question.

"What is the Association?" he asked.

"It hasn't been this good in years," she said. "Not since him." She waved vaguely in the direction of a box on top of her small night table.

"The Association," Remo repeated.

"Must we talk now?" she said. "Can you do some more of that stuff with the back of the left knee?"

"No," said Remo. "Definitely not. That was step eighteen and I'm up to step twenty-nine. If I go back to step eighteen, I'll have to start up all over again from there. I might be here all night."

"Would that be so bad?"

"Not if we had something to talk about," Remo said. "Like the Association. Who's the Association? What is it?"

"It's our national group to preserve the environment," she said. "Keep going."

133

Step thirty.

"Then why would they want to kill anybody?" Remo asked.

"Kill? Them? Remo, stop it. They can't even fuck. How can they kill?"

"Well, who's doing all the killing down at the Tulsa Torrent project?"

"Got me," Cicely Winston-Alright said.

"What a waste of time," Remo said. He pulled back from the woman.

"Remo," she said, "would you do me a favor?"

"A small one," Remo said.

"Take me outside and do it in the snow, under the trees. I love doing it amid nature. It feels so good, so natural. Please."

"I guess so," Remo said.

"I like trees," she said. "They're so . . . so . . . symbolic," she said.

"Terrific," he said. Thirty steps wasted and he hadn't found anything out, and this woman was still as stiff from hip to knee as she had been when he had first seen her.

He lifted her up and carried her out the back door of the trailer. He dumped her roughly on the ground. For the first time she squealed, and it was an honest squeal of passion.

"Just jump on me and bang away," she said. "Forget technique."

Remo followed her instructions, landing on her roughly, pushing her arms far apart, pinning them down with his strong hands, pressing hard enough to bruise her creamy skin, and inside ten seconds the woman melted, trembling and quaking, shuddering with the intense release of passion.

134

She lay still under him, her shoulders trembling slightly against the snow.

"That was marvelous," she said.

"Why didn't you tell me you liked rough stuff?" he said. "I could have saved a lot of time."

"I like rough stuff. Save time."

So they did it again. And again.

The third time, Remo asked her again: "Who's behind the killings?"

"I don't know," she said.

"What's the Association?"

"Ecology group. Pays our bills."

"Swell," Remo growled. He stood up and looked down at her. "You better get inside before you catch cold."

She nodded. "Will you come and keep me warm again?"

"Absolutely," he said. "On June 17th, I'm free from eight till nine in the morning."

"I'll wait," she said, as Remo crunched off through the snow, leaving her lying on the ground.

Cicely Winston-Alright went back into her trailer and closed the door behind her, then leaned up against it. God, she thought, at last a man . . . someone who wasn't put off by her money or her beauty and wasn't afraid just to take her like an animal in the woods. She could feel a shiver down her back. She was still throbbing *down there*, for the first time in years. Only one other man had ever . . . it was just like in the movies . . . like the books she sneaked out of her mother's closet . . .

She sighed and wondered if Remo had left yet. She

135

ran to the front window of the trailer and looked out into the clearing, but he had gone.

She smiled and ran her fingers over her body. He would be back, she thought. She would make sure that he came back. If only men knew that she wanted them to be men, that she wanted them to take her, to force her, to bend her to their will, to hurt her. Why didn't men ever realize?

She walked to her bed and put on a flimsy black peignoir. Then she heard a sound in her kitchen, at the other end of the trailer behind a thin plywood door.

It was short, dark, and pretty Ararat Carpathian. God, how she hated Armenians, she thought. Not that she knew that many. In fact, Carpathian was the only one she knew, but she hated him enough to make up for all the rest. If they could only find some way of boiling down those people, she thought, America could solve its oil problems by breeding Armenians.

She smiled at him and let her gown slip open slightly, making sure he got a good view of her front, then slowly pulled it closed.

"Why, Ari," she said. "How nice to see you."

"I've been waiting quite a while," Carpathian said. "But you were busy."

"Oh, you noticed," she said. "Yes. Quite busy."

"Your friend seemed to want to talk," Carpathian said.

"Men always do," she said. She busied herself at the stove, making a cup of hot chocolate. She did not offer him any. When she turned to come and join him at the kitchen table, she noticed for the first time that he had a lumberjack's double-bladed axe leaning up against the wall behind his seat.

"Well, what is on your mind, Ari?" she asked.

136

"Tonight's demonstration," he said.

"Ah, yes. The demonstration. We seem to live and die by our demonstrations, don't we, Ari?"

She noticed him smirking under the thin line of his mustache.

"You could say that, Cicely," he said.

She wondered why he was carrying that axe around.

"Our people are beginning to feel uneasy," Ari said. "After last night's fiasco and with the press watching, they're losing their enthusiasm for tonight."

"Go make a speech. That'll whip them up."

"No. They need more than that," he said.

Mrs. Winston-Alright shook her head from side to side.

"Well, go give them something more. You can't expect me to do everything, can you?"

"This is something only you can give them," Ari said. He shifted in his chair and she saw his hand move for the handle of the axe.

"Oh? What is that?" she said, sipping her chocolate. Maybe he wanted to rape her, maybe this poor insignificant little twerp had always longed for her body; maybe his manners and his deference and his courtliness hadn't worked and now he had decided to take her by force to satisfy his lust. She felt herself going wet again. She wouldn't fight. No woman was ever hurt by a good rape.

"Go ahead," she said. "I won't resist."

"You won't?" he said. "You know what's on my mind?

"Yes, you savage Armenian beast. You've come to rape me. Well, go ahead. Although what that's got to do with tonight's demonstration, I'll never know."

"Actually, nothing," he said coldly. "And that's not what's on my mind."

"It isn't?" Without realizing it, she had slipped down in her chair, and now Cicely Winston-Alright sat up straight again. She looked at him with a dowager empress's commanding eye.

"What then do our people need tonight?" she said, trying to get her mind back to business.

"I've talked to our backers at the Association," Ararat Carpathian said. "They agree with me. Totally."

"Agree with what?"

"That we need a martyr."

"A what?" she asked.

"We need a martyr. We need someone to be the victim of a gory, grisly murder—a particularly horrible, bloody thing that we can blame on the people of Tulsa Torrent. That'll bring out the marchers."

She sighed. "I suppose so, if that's what the Association thinks."

"I'm glad you feel that way."

Carpathian picked up the double-bladed axe and set it on the table.

"That's what I got this for, Cicely."

"I see," she said, and shuddered visibly.

"It should be most effective for our purposes," he said softly.

"I suppose so. But I hate to look at it." It was funny, she thought; she had never realized how much the little man's eyes looked like a cobra's. They were almost hypnotizing.

Ari stood up and took the axe in hand, almost as if he were about to chop a log.

"That thing gives me the creeps," she said.

"It won't for long."

138

"Have you picked your victim yet?" she asked. She looked in his eyes. His eyes held her. She had her answer without his saying a word. She wanted to scream but couldn't.

Finally, he answered her. "Yes, Cicely. I have."

It took him ten chops to get exactly the effect he wanted.

CHAPTER FOURTEEN

The moon was high in the sky when Remo came back across the snow to Alpha Camp. There was a large mound of snow where the A-frame building had been, and the air still carried the faint aroma of burnt wood, an aroma faintly redolent to Remo of his childhood days in Newark when he and some friends would start a fire in a vacant lot, then throw in raw potatoes to char them black. The burnt potato skins gave off that woody smell.

Remo was thinking of Cicely Winston-Alright as he walked past the mound that had been the A-frame, when suddenly he felt a pair of strong arms surround him, and a heavy weight bear him to the ground.

"Gotcha, you bet," he heard the French-accented voice roar in his ear.

"Goddammit, Pierre, it's me," he said.

Remo had a mouthful of snow. He felt the big weight get off his back, then a strong hand pulled him to his feet.

"Peer sorry," the big man told Remo. "But you sneak across the snow like an Indian, and Peer think it somebody coming back to make trouble."

"All right," Remo said. "No harm done." He realized how much Sinanju had become a part of him. He

141

had not been sneaking back to camp; he had just been strolling. But his stroll today was a soundless, ghostlike movement, beyond the ability of an ordinary man. He was glad that Pierre LaRue was alert.

The two men went inside the log cabin bunkhouse. Chiun and Joey Webb were sitting on a couch. Chiun was sipping daintily from a cup of tea. Joey's hands held a big tea mug, and from time to time she took a big gulp from it. The fireplace gave off the only light and heat in the room, and the young woman seemed to be vacillating between moving closer to it and pulling away from it. Pierre went to a corner and sat his big body down in an old rocking chair. A cat that had been hiding under the chair scurried out into a dark corner.

Looking at Joey, Remo thought about how much the girl had gone through in the last few weeks and how close to the edge of breaking she must be.

Joey looked up at Remo as he stepped into the jagged circle of light thrown off by the fire.

She smiled a hello to him, and he nodded back.

"Everything all right down with the copa-ibas?" he asked.

She said something in answer, but Remo didn't hear it.

He had turned to face the fireplace and let his mind go out to embrace the flames. For the next two minutes, he thought of nothing but his breathing and the rhythm of his blood as it coursed through his body.

When he came back from his rhythm fix, he saw Joey standing next to the fireplace. An old-fashioned standing hook was set into one side of it, and suspended from the hook was an equally old-fashioned teapot.

"Would you like some tea?" she asked him

Remo hesitated. Since he had been brought, kicking

and screaming, into the House of Sinanju, his body had changed. He could no longer eat as he once did: Additives could kill him; most food made him want to throw up. His body was too closely tuned, too sensitive to sensation, to tolerate the garbage that most Americans compacted into their mouths. He was hesitant even to try other people's tea.

"It is not bad tea," said Chiun.

"For an American?" Remo asked.

"For an American, it is excellent tea," Chiun said. "For a Korean, it is not bad."

"Good. Then I'll have some," Remo said.

"Same way, right. No sugar, no milk, no lemon, no anything," she told him

"Right," Remo agreed.

"I never could drink it that way," she said. She began to stutter slightly and then stopped. "Oscar always drank his the same way."

"Don't dwell on it, kid," Remo said, rising to take the cup from her. "What's done is done."

"I know." She made an obvious attempt to be more cheerful. "And now for the good news."

"All right," Remo said. "What's the good news?"

"We've figured out how to solve the problem of making the copa-ibas grow in this climate. Or, at least, I think we have."

"Great," Remo said, "How'd you do that?" Behind him, he heard Pierre LaRue lean forward on the rocking chair to listen.

"Actually, Chiun figured it out."

"It was nothing," Chiun said. Remo nodded agreement. Chiun added, "For me, that is. For Remo, it would have been impossible, because it involved thinking."

Joey reached out and touched Chiun's hand good-humoredly. For a fraction of a second, Remo thought he could see a flicker of pride pass through the old man's eyes.

"So what's the solution?" Remo asked. "Or maybe I better ask first, what was the problem?"

"The problem has always been that copa-iba is a tropical tree," Joey said.

"Not Korean?" asked Remo, with a serious face.

"We have resolved that satisfactorily," Chiun said. "Probably the tree was brought from Korea to Brazil many thousands of years ago. Then it was brought to this country."

Remo nodded. "Got it," he said.

"With a tropical tree," Joey said, "there's practically no place in the continental U.S. where we can grow them, except for a little fringe on the Texas gulf coast and a little tiny bit of southern Florida."

"So the problem is trying to find a way to make them grow up here in this dismal climate," Remo said. "That's why all the blowers and the fans and heaters?"

"That's right," she said.

"Does it work?"

"In a way," Joey said. "I mean, we can grow the trees that way. No doubt about it. But it's not worth it. We use more oil and gasoline to run the equipment than the oil we can get out of the trees. The only reason we've been keeping it going is to have some adult trees to study."

"Then the experiment was a flop?" Remo said.

"No. I didn't say that. The big breakthrough was about six months ago. After all this time of planning and trying and fooling around, we finally discovered a way to get the copa-iba seeds to sprout quickly. It used

144

to take thirty to forty years for a single seed to germinate. Now we can get it to do that in only three or four weeks. That was the first breakthrough."

"How do you do it?" Remo asked.

Joey walked back to the fire. Behind him, Pierre was still not rocking, Remo noticed.

"I'm not sure I should tell you," Joey said.

"I think you should. It might help us figure out what's going on around here," Remo said.

"What do you mean?"

"I mean that people didn't start dying until your breakthrough with getting seeds to sprout or whatever."

Joey hesitated for a moment. "Maybe," she said. "Anyway, all I do is soak the seeds in this special mixture I've developed. And it works. It really works."

"And who else knew about this mixture besides you?"

"Knows it exists?" asked Joey.

"Yes."

"A hundred people at Tulsa Torrent," she said.

"Who knew what was in it?" asked Remo.

"Just Danny and Oscar and me."

"And now they're dead and somebody's trying to kill you," Remo said.

"It looks that way," she said.

"Why is this so important?" Remo asked. "So who cares if seeds whatchamacallit in weeks or years?"

"It speeds up research. Look. Suppose we grow a hundred trees and two of them seem to have a special resistance to cold. Well, we can take those trees and cross-fertilize them and plant them and get a lot more trees and maybe if you're lucky a lot of them will be more resistant to the cold. And you keep doing it. But if you can only get seeds every thirty years, it's going to take you centuries to make a dent. That's why my breakthrough was so important; now we can speed up the research program."

"I see. Now what does Chiun have to do with all this marvelous wisdom?" Remo said.

"Black silk and spacing," she said. "It's just so obvious none of us ever thought of it."

"You should have asked me," Remo said. "The first thing I think about in the morning is black silk and spacing."

Chiun snorted. Joey laughed.

"What are you talking about, black silk and spacing?" Remo asked.

"The bottom line here is to get these trees growing in this northern climate. We know with enough time we're going to build a super-tree that can thrive up here. But what about in the meantime? All we've been able to figure out is this dumb heating system that uses fifty gallons of oil to make maybe a quart in a tree. Chiun's found a better way to grow the trees."

"It was easy," Chiun said. "In my village of Sinanju, everybody knows things like that. Except white people who visit occasionally. They don't know anything."

"What Chiun said was this," Joey explained. "Thin out the copa-ibas. Then in the spaces between and around them, plant pine trees. Cover the ground under the trees with black silk with vents cut in it. Now, what happens is that the needles fall off the pine trees, through the vents in the silk, and pile up on the ground. With a watering system, you keep them wet. The black silk absorbs sunlight and heat, and helps build a giant compost heap under all the trees. Then the vents let out heat and moisture. This keeps the copa-iba trees warm and wet, just as they are in Brazil. What it does is to

146

use the pine trees to create artificial environment that can keep the copa-ibas alive anywhere in the world."

"Will it work?" Remo said.

"I think so," she said. "I'm sure it will. As soon as the winter breaks, we're going to give it a try. It's a brilliant idea."

"I could have thought of that," Remo said. "It was just that no one ever explained the problem to me. It's obvious. The first thing to do would have been to use black silk. Anybody knows that."

"Well, Chiun told me. He's so wise," Joey said.

"He is something, that's for sure," Remo said.

Behind him, he heard Pierre LaRue get to his feet, yawn elaborately, and walk toward them.

"Peer turn in," he said. "A long night last night."

Joey wished him good night, Remo nodded, and Chiun ignored the big Frenchman as he stomped heavily out the front door.

But sleep was not on Pierre LaRue's mind.

Once outside the bunkhouse, he started through the woods, down the hillside to the road, and along the road toward the Mountain High group's encampment and the luxuriously appointed trailer of Mrs. Cicely Winston-Alright. It was Thursday night and he had made the trip every Thursday night for the past three months, ever since the Mountain Highs had arrived to harass this station of the Tulsa Torrent company.

He remembered that first night. He was too bone-tired to do anything except chug down a few beers and collapse into bed, and she had come up to him in the little tavern in the village down below and asked him to dance.

He asked her who she was, and she replied that she was the enemy. She had come to put him and his company out of business. She was a lady, a very important lady—no doubt about it—and he had not even had time to put on a clean shirt after his day's work, much less shower and splash himself with cologne. But it didn't matter to her. They danced, and he tried to reason with her. He explained why Tulsa Torrent was a good company that actually improved the land, by making it more fertile, and growing more trees than they cut down. But she ground her body against his and said she had heard all the arguments, and she was still against the company.

Then she took him back to her trailer and did things to his body that he had only read about in books, and then he spent the rest of the night acting like a battering ram. In the morning, he could barely move; he was so stiff and tired he slept-walked through his day's work. But she had told him she wanted him back the following Thursday.

And she insisted that he not shower first.

So he came to her without washing the sweat from his body and never once would she let him out of her arms while they were together. If they even snacked at night, they did it while their loins were still locked, one into the other.

But tonight, Pierre LaRue was not looking forward to lovemaking. The things that Joey had said about being the last one alive who knew how to make the copa-iba seeds grow faster made him uncomfortable, particularly with the growing craziness of the Mountain Highs.

He would reason with Mrs. Winston-Alright tonight

148

and ask her to pack up her band of followers and go home, and the first one she should send away was that oily little assistant of hers. The man's name was Ararat, and the woman always called him Ari. But to Pierre, the man was Arat. As he walked through the moonlight and the snow, Pierre laughed aloud. Arat was a good name for the man, he thought, because that was what the little fellow was: a rat.

When LaRue got to Mrs. Winston-Alright's trailer and knocked on the back door, he was surprised to see Arat open the door. The little man smiled at him; he looked so greasy that Pierre thought if he gave him one good squeeze, the man would ooze juice.

"Ah, Pierre," the small man said. "How nice to see you again."

LaRue mumbled an acknowledgment.

"Cicely's waiting for you in the back room," the man said.

Pierre stepped inside the trailer and walked toward the small bedroom in the back. He heard the steps of the small man behind him. The door to the bedroom was closed. Pierre opened it, then stopped short, in horror, as the butchered pieces of Cicely Winston-Alright's body, strewn onto the bedspread, filled him with fear and shock.

He wheeled to face the little man.

Ararat Carpathian raised Mrs. Winston-Alright's little silver-plated revolver and shot the big Frenchman in the chest twice.

Pierre fell like one of his beloved trees.

The small man took the double-bladed axe from behind the door and carefully fitted it into the dead lumberjack's huge hands.

Then he searched carefully to find Mrs. Winston-Alright's right hand, put the gun in it and dropped it onto the floor.

Having completed his mission, Ararat Carpathian fled from the trailer.

CHAPTER FIFTEEN

The bunkhouse was quiet. Joey Webb slept curled like a two-year-old on a fur rug in front of the fire. Not far away, Chiun sat on the floor, legs folded under him. He had managed to confiscate some paper and an old fountain pen from the desk, and despite grumbling that it was impossible for a civilized man to write with junk and toys, he was busy writing another chapter for the History of Sinanju. Now that Joey had explained to him how he may have saved the Western world from the Arab oil threat by discovering how to make the copa-ibas grow, Chiun thought that all generations to come should know of this.

He had tentatively entitled the chapter: "Chiun Saves the Barbarians."

Remo sat in a chair, watching Chiun.

The telephone rang. It was a soft ring, and Joey did not even stir in her sleep. Chiun said, "It is becoming impossible to work with all these interruptions. Please answer that thing."

"Let it ring," Remo said.

"Answer it," Chiun commanded.

Remo walked over to the telephone. He half expected Smith's acid voice to bite at him over the phone, but instead the voice was one he had not expected.

It was an oily, insidious half-whisper, hissing "Remo, Remo, Remo." It was the same voice Remo had found on the tape recorder the night before.

"Who is this?" Remo said.

The faraway voice ignored the question. Instead it hissed, "LaRue needs you. At Cicely's trailer. Hurry, Remo."

"Who is this?" Remo said again. The voice was familiar but not familiar—as if it were a voice he had heard before but talking through a series of baffles that changed its pitch and rhythm.

The telephone clicked in his ear.

"I have to go," Remo told Chiun.

"Good. Take the telephone with you," Chiun said.

Remo pushed off through the woods, jogging up to the road, and then down toward the Mountain High encampment. Of course, it was a trap. He knew that. But right now, walking into a trap might be his best lead, his only way out of the dead-end of this puzzle.

Still, he was on his guard as he moved toward the clearing that the Mountain Highs infested.

The first thing he noticed was the silence. Before, there had been people moving around inside the tents, talking, cooking, making love. Now, there was only stillness. He moved into the shadow of a tree to look over the area.

Off in the far left corner of the clearing, he saw a cluster of three people. They were holding portable lights and camera equipment. Remo was puzzled. Apparently what they wanted was to film him. But why? And what about Pierre LaRue? How was he involved?

In the cluster of people in the far corner, he recognized the oily little man who was Cicely Winston-Alright's aide. Some kind of setup, he thought again.

Remo pushed his way quietly along the edge of the clearing, watching for movement, traveling noiselessly across the top of the snow. When the trailer was between him and the cluster of people, Remo dropped to the snow and, skittering across its surface like a crab across sand, slid under the trailer.

Quietly he moved to the far end of the trailer. In the shadows, he could not be seen. He heard their voices.

"Be ready," he heard the oily man say. "When he goes in, we'll set up, and then when he comes out, we'll film him. Then we'll move right into the trailer and film inside."

"What's inside that's such a big deal?" someone asked.

"You'll see," the oily man said.

Remo moved back to the far end of the trailer. He would be just about under the kitchen, he figured. He reached up with both hands and felt one of the metal panels that provided the sub-flooring for the trailer. He slammed out with the spear of a hardened fingertip and punched a hole into the thin steel. There was one muffled thump and then silence. He waited. No one had heard. The three people in the corner of the clearing kept whispering to each other.

Carefully, Remo extended the hole in the steel, until it was large enough for both his hands to dig into. Then he carefully, slowly, and quietly ripped out the panel and set it on the ground. Above him, the flooring was a series of plywood squares, covered, he remembered, with nine-inch-square vinyl tiles. Remo used the heel of his hand to thump up against the plywood. It gave immediately, and a wedge of space opened up into the trailer above. Remo waited for a few moments to make sure no one had heard, then moved through the narrow opening up into the trailer.

The structure was dark, but light filtering in from outdoors made it seem as bright as daylight to Remo.

He moved toward Cicely Winston-Alright's bedroom at the far end of the trailer. On the floor, in the doorway, he saw Pierre LaRue. He bent down next to the man. He saw the bullet wounds in the chest. There was a faint pulse in LaRue's neck and as he touched it, Remo heard the big Frenchman groan softly.

There was nothing Remo could do. Perhaps if he had come ten minutes sooner. But too much blood had been lost.

Remo tried to make him comfortable.

"Pierre, who did this?" he asked.

"A rat," LaRue said. "A rat did zees. And inside, too."

"Worse than a rat," Remo said, not understanding.

"A rat," LaRue said. In the dimness, his eyes pleaded for understanding, for comprehension on Remo's part. "A rat. A rat."

He bubbled blood for a few seconds, then his lips turned blue. His hands began to slash and his eyes rolled back in his head. Pierre LaRue died.

What had he meant, "Inside, too"? Remo stood up and looked into the bedroom. He found Cicely. There was no need to check to see if she were dead. There weren't any pieces big enough to sustain life.

Remo understood now why the men were outside. They wanted to film him and LaRue and the woman. They were going to blame her death on Tulsa Torrent, perhaps use it all to kick off a riot that could sweep like a flood through the Tulsa Torrent land and destroy the copa-ibas.

Remo was angry. He had liked LaRue.

He lifted LaRue in his arms and brought him back to the trapdoor he had cut in the kitchen floor. Gently, as if the man were still alive, he lowered him down to the ground.

Then he went back to get LaRue's axe. He dropped it, too, through the opening. For a moment, he considered disposing also of Cicely's butchered body, but decided it was too messy. He let himself back down through the kitchen floor, then pulled the plywood and tile back into place from below. He bent up the ripped steel panel.

He had the feeling that he was forgetting something, something he should check. It gnawed at him, but he shrugged it off and scrambled to the end of the trailer, pulling Pierre LaRue's body after him.

Once he got out from under the structure, he hoisted Pierre LaRue into his arms, grabbed the double-faced axe in his right hand, and moved off silently into the safe darkness of the trees.

As he walked back through the woods toward Alpha Camp, Remo could feel Pierre's body growing cold in his arms. Remo stopped on the hill overlooking the valley of copa-iba trees. The heat from the generators and blowers moved up around them, along with the scent of gasoline and the noise of motors. Remo shook his head. Was it all worth it? Were these trees worth so many lives? Were they worth the life of this big, glorious, happy Frenchman he carried in his arms?

Gently, Remo lay Pierre down in the snow, and with his hands he covered over the man's body. There would be time for burying later, and this would be the spot, among the trees that LaRue loved. Dragging the big woodsman's axe behind him, Remo went back to the log cabin. When he reached Alpha Camp, he drew his arm back and angrily slung the axe, end over end, across the clearing. The blade hit clean and buried itself three inches deep into the trunk of a ponderosa pine.

Chiun was still sitting where Remo had left him.

He looked up as Remo came in. "I am glad you are here," he said. "Should I call this chapter 'Chiun Saves the Barbarians' or 'Chiun Saves Everybody'?"

"Who the hell cares?" Remo said.

"That is a stupid title," Chiun said.

But Remo wasn't listening. He was on the telephone, dialing Smith. It was after midnight on the East Coast, but Remo knew that did not matter. When Remo was off on an assignment, Smith could almost always be found in his office.

He was there now.

"Don't you ever sleep?" Remo asked.

"How is that relevant?" Smith asked.

"Never mind," Remo said. Quickly, he filled him in on the death of Pierre LaRue and Mrs. Winston-Alright.

"Did he kill her?" Smith asked.

"I don't think so. I think somebody else did, then bushwhacked him, and was trying to wrap the frame all in a neat package by getting pictures of me, too."

"That might be," Smith agreed. "What did he mean 'A rat did this'?"

"I don't know. Have you found out anything about the dead men? The tape recorder? The Mountain Highs?"

"That is why I'm waiting here," Smith said. "The computer has not yet finished scanning its memories."

"Swell," Remo growled. "People are getting swatted

around here like flies, and we're waiting for some big goddamn machine to finish scanning its memories."

"I will call as soon as I have anything," Smith said blandly.

Remo slammed the phone down onto the base. He looked to Chiun, but before he could speak, the telephone rang.

"What now?" he growled into the mouthpiece, thinking it was Smith calling back.

It was Roger Stacy.

"What the hell is going on?" Stacy demanded.

"What are you talking about?" Remo said.

"I've just heard that those Mountain High lunatics are massing down at their camp. They're screaming murder and protests and who knows what else. You murder somebody?"

"Not yet," Remo said coldly. "Stacy, I want you to send some guards down here."

"What for?"

"To guard Joey. I'm going to be out."

"All right. They're on their way. But listen, O'Sylvan . . ."

"What?"

"Don't cause any trouble."

By the time Remo and Chiun reached the encampment of the Mountain High Society, carnival time had begun. The night before, the society had had only a hundred demonstrators in its candlelight march, but already, more than five hundred people had swelled the small camping ground. With them came a full complement of entertainers, souvenir vendors, and instant health-food snack bars set up by local impresarios who knew nut cases when they saw them.

As Remo and Chiun moved through the crowd, Chiun was besieged by pimply-faced sixteen-year-olds and face-lifted thirty-eight-year-olds looking for guidance and wisdom. He told each in Korean that they were lower than snake droppings. Each accepted this bit of Oriental wisdom and went off enriched.

Remo was listening to snatches of conversation. Something big was supposed to happen. Something big was going to be announced.

"What's happening?" Remo asked a young woman whose shirt proclaimed that she liked dogs better than men, apparently having sampled both.

"The fascists have gone too far this time," she said.

"What's that mean?" Remo asked her.

"I don't know. That's what I was told," she said.

Remo moved off. He heard other rumors. That the police were going to arrest all the demonstrators; that Tulsa Torrent goon squads were going to use tear gas, mace, and nerve gas against the demonstrators just to protect their filthy profits. Both these rumors were generally believed. A third was offered up as just a rumor, probably groundless. According to this least believable rumor, one of the leaders of the Mountain High Society had been hacked to pieces by a Tulsa Torrent lumberjack.

A makeshift stage had been set up. A trio of superannuated, beatnik folk singers who had never been known to miss a paying date climbed onto the stage and began running through a catalog of their greatest hits from twenty years before. The crowd began pressing forward. Remo and Chiun moved along with them.

After the crowd had been warmed up, Ararat Carpathian came onto the bandstand. Remo recognized him as Cicely Winston-Alright's aide-de-camp and heard the people around him call the curly-haired man's name. "Ari. Ari. Ari." Then he heard others yell "A rat. A rat. A rat."

"What are they yelling?" he asked a nearly hoarse young woman who was screaming the name with almost religious fervor.

"Arat," she said.

"That's not a nice thing to call him," Remo said.

"That's his name. Ararat Carpathian. He's Mrs. Winston-Alright's right-hand man. We call him Arat."

"Oh," said Remo, remembering Pierre LaRue's last words. "Thank you."

"That's okay," the woman said. "Anyone ever tell you you've got nifty dark eyes?"

"No," Remo said. "You're the very first."

"That's him," Remo told Chiun. "He's the one who killed LaRue." He muttered to himself: "A rat. A rat."

Carpathian had raised his arms for quiet and the crowd followed his lead.

"Friends," he yelled into a microphone. "I have bad news."

There was a groan from the audience.

"Our leader, the beloved Cicely Winston-Alright, is dead."

There were screams of anguish from the crowd, sobs, shouts of disbelief.

"This loving woman, who so loved us and so loved the good earth, was struck down in the prime of her life by a murderer most vicious and foul," Carpathian bellowed.

The crowd surged forward as if physically expressing its anger.

"Who did it? Who? Who?" the crowd screamed.

"The pig police have not arrested anyone yet, but we know who did it," Carpathian said.

"Who? Who? Who?"

"A lumberjack for Tulsa Torrent. A lumberjack probably insane with guilt from the crazy demands of his job. Or else just one whose palm was greased with blood money."

Remo and Chiun moved closer to the speaker's platform. Ararat Carpathian screamed, "Are we going to let them get away with it?"

The crowd screamed *no, no, no,* in one long, full-throated yell. Carpathian looked down and below his feet saw Chiun and Remo. He saw Remo smile and raise one finger, pointing it squarely at Carpathian's chest. The man's smile was cold as death.

Carpathian moved back from the microphone. By the time Remo brushed aside the crowd and hopped up onto the platform, Carpathian was gone and nowhere to be seen. Remo turned just as the crowd began charging the speaker's platform, deciding to take out their frustrated anger on their own property.

Remo looked around. He saw Carpathian's back disappearing through the trees across the road. Remo walked through the small glade of trees and into a clearing on the other side. A dozen snowmobiles were parked there. Carpathian was sitting astride one of them, talking to Harvey Quibble, the government inspector.

Remo called out: "A rat."

Carpathian looked around. He saw Remo. Then he seemed to slump forward over the controls of his machine, and the snowmobile jumped into action, driving straight ahead down a snow-covered trail.

Remo ran off after it. He had almost caught up with Carpathian when the trail made a sharp right-hand turn. Carpathian's snowmobile did not. Instead, it kept going straight ahead, plunging through a dense tangle of low underbrush and then out and over a hundred-foot-high drop-off.

By the time Remo got to him, Ararat Carpathian was little more than a sausage skin filled with once-human jelly.

CHAPTER SIXTEEN

Company guards and the town police arrived just before the disorderly gang of protesters could turn into a surging mob, and slowly herded them back into the protesters' camping grounds.

Arriving with the police was Roger Stacy, who walked away from the mob scene, went through the thin bank of trees, and entered the clearing where Remo was approaching Harvey Quibble.

Quibble saw Stacy approaching, and he pointed a long, tremulous finger at Remo and squeaked, "He did it again. I saw him with my very own two eyes. This . . . this ersatz tree inspector chased that poor man over the side of the cliff." As Remo drew near, Quibble drew himself up to his full height. "You, sir, are not merely an imcompetent," he said, "you are a murderer." He turned to Stacy. "He is, he is," he said.

"Shove it," said Remo.

Stacy looked from Quibble to Remo, from Quibble to Remo, then back to Quibble again.

"I'm sure Mr. O'Sylvan didn't kill anybody," he said. He turned once again to Remo. "Did you?"

Remo said nothing. He saw Chiun approaching from across the road. Behind them, the police were setting up barricades penning in the protesters.

"See," Quibble said. "What did I tell you? He won't even dialog with us. We have no room on the government team for these kind of people . . . these killers. I don't care how much you may miss him, Mr. Stacy, but after I contact Washington tomorrow, this Remo O'Sylvan is going to be off the job." Quibble puffed out his tiny sparrow's chest.

"I told you, shove it," Remo said. "He was dead before I ever reached him."

"How do you know that?" Stacy said.

"I don't believe it," Quibble said.

"He didn't scream," Remo said. "He went ass over teakettle off the edge of a hundred-foot cliff and he didn't scream. He was either dead or unconscious already."

"Oh," said Stacy.

"You can give that lame excuse to the personnel department," Quibble said, "but my report goes in as I saw it."

The federal job inspector and Stacy began a heated argument and Remo, disgusted, walked over to Chiun. The old man was sniffing the air.

"They're using tear gas," Remo said.

Chiun shook his head. "Not that," he said. "Something else. Something sweet."

As he and Chiun disappeared into the woods, Remo looked back. Stacy and Harvey Quibble were still arguing.

No one challenged Remo and Chiun as they went back to the log cabin. When they went inside, Joey Webb was sitting in front of the fire, reading.

"What happened?" she asked Remo quickly. "Tell me all about it."

165

"Nothing happened. Where're the guards that were supposed to be here?"

"I don't know," Joey said. "I didn't see any guards."

"I told that horse's ass Stacy to send guards down here," Remo snarled.

"I'm all right. Stop worrying. What happened up there?"

Remo thought of telling her about Cicely Winston-Alright, about Carpathian, and about Pierre LaRue's death earlier in the night; but he decided not to—the girl had had enough to worry about in the past weeks, and the rush of events of the last twenty-four hours might be enough to snap her spirit, no matter how strong.

"Nothing much happened," Remo repeated as he walked to the telephone. "A lot of speeches, yakety-yak, the cops broke up the march, and that was that."

"Oh, you got a phone call," Joey Webb said.

"Who was it?"

"I think it was Dr. Smith. He said you are to call your Aunt Mildred."

"That was Smitty. I don't have an Aunt Mildred," Remo said.

He took the phone with him into the corner of the room and dialed Smith's direct number.

"Yes?" came Smith's voice.

"What was it? You called."

"The two dead men were Rhodesian nationals. They had no history in this country. Salisbury police suspect they might have been contract killers, but there is no firm evidence either way."

Remo nodded. "It's safe to assume that if they were here, they were here working for somebody," he said.

"That's right," Smith said.

"How about the Mountain High Society?" Remo asked.

"I don't know about that," said Smith. "Hiring killers would not seem to be their style. Basically, they have been just another one of hundreds of protest groups. Perhaps a little better financed than most organizations like that, but otherwise not much different."

"How about their leadership? That broad with two names. That little greaseball Carpathian?"

"Both clean," Smith said.

"Both dead, too," Remo said.

"Oh," said Smith. Quickly Remo told him what had happened, without mentioning Pierre LaRue, trying to keep his voice down so that Joey could not hear him.

"Mrs. Winston-Alright was one of the founders of the society," Smith said. "And until a few years ago, she bankrolled it."

"And then what happened?" Remo asked.

"Her second husband, Lance Alright, left her. He left her penniless. There was a suspicion that he took her money and ran off to indulge in oil speculation. Nothing's been heard of him since."

"She didn't live like she was poor," Remo said.

"I don't know. She had no income. Carpathian drifted into this society right after graduating college. It upset his family, who are wealthy merchants in the Middle East."

"Oil. Middle East," Remo mused aloud. "What about the tape recorder? Anything?"

"A cheap type made by the hundreds of thousands. Most of this particular model was bought up by the federal government for its own use. I'm still trying to track down the specific model."

"Keep in touch," Remo said. He hung up, disappointed. The bodies were piling to the sky, and still there was no hard information, no solid lead. Just a lot of unanswered questions.

He vowed that he would not leave Joey Webb alone or out of his sight, until everything was cleared up.

Remo was wakened by Chiun standing over him.

"What's wrong?" Remo asked, instantly awake.

"The forest is afire," Chiun said.

Remo jumped to his feet. "Those damn Mountain Highs," he snarled as he ran to the front door.

"Perhaps," Chiun said.

The two men went outside. To the north, the hillside was an undulating wall of flame. To the west and east and south, it was the same. The woods were filled with smoke and mist as the fire ate its way down the hillsides toward the valley in which Alpha camp and the grove of copa-ibas sat.

"We're surrounded," Remo said.

"Exactly," Chiun said.

"What about Joey?" Remo said. There was no need for him to explain to Chiun that they could escape, but fighting their way through the fire could mean the young woman scientist's life.

Even as they spoke, the area around the log cabin began to turn into a maelstrom of sparks. Nearby, they could hear the thud of falling limbs from trees and the explosion of vehicles and bulldozers and tree-yanking machines that were parked all through the forest.

Joey met them at the door, rubbing her eyes.

"Oh, Christ," she said. "How the hell do we get out of here?"

"If we want to save the copa-ibas, we don't," Remo

said. He looked at Chiun, almost helplessly. "Everything is burning."

"Not everything," Chiun said.

Remo stopped and looked. Around them, the fire was moving down the mountainsides like syrup down the side of a bowl. Trees were burning. Outbuildings. Logging equipment. What was not burning?

The snow.

The snow was not burning.

He nodded to Chiun, and together he and the old man began to pile up snow. They built a mound in the center of the biggest clearing in front of the camp buildings. When they had dug out a big hollow, Remo told Joey, "Get in."

"What?" she exclaimed.

"Just get inside that snow wall." The girl, frightened now by the growing insidious crackle of the flames, gulped, nodded, and obeyed. Quickly, Remo and Chiun built a sloping roof of snow over the structure. The girl was sealed off from the flames. Hopefully, the igloo would last long enough for them to do their work. She was safe. Now save the copa-ibas. Then save themselves.

"What now, Chiun?" Remo said.

"Just follow," the Oriental said.

The old man's plan of attack was simple. "Every tree," he said, "wants to fall over on its side as much as it wants to stand up straight. We will help them."

They moved up the north side of the sloping mountain, until they were only fifty yards ahead of the main wall of fire, which was swooping down the mountainside, leapfrogging from burning tree to burning tree. As Remo watched, Chiun felt the side of a tree trunk,

169

searching with his hands for the point of critical balance. Then, with a push that was almost childlike, Chiun pressed against the tree, and with a ripping, cracking sound, the big timber toppled to the ground.

Remo understood. He and Chiun flashed along the line of trees, pushing them over. Big trees took down smaller trees. Slowly, they were creating a clearing, in which toppled trees were piled one on top of another. As the flames coming down the hillside met that wall, there would be no more standing trees for the flames to jump to. The fire would burn itself down toward ihe ground and ignite the fallen trees, but it would be a slow process, and the fire would not have enough energy to jump across the firebreak.

Without resting, without waiting, Chiun kept working his way around the rim of the bowl of the mountain. Remo raced ahead, leveling a broad swath of timber, then would feel Chiun run past him to do the same thing ahead. They leapfrogged their way around the entire mountain, cutting a wide path through the standing pines.

Finally, after two hours, they moved back down the hill toward Alpha Camp.

As they looked up, around them, 360 degrees, they could see that already the fire was slowing, running into the wall of felled trees, unable to jump that wall, and now turning its energy away from expansion, and in upon itself, consuming itself, slowly burning itself out.

They decided to leave Joey in the igloo. She would be safe there until they came back.

Roger Stacy was leaning back in his swivel chair, playing with the gold-plated steel lumberjack's hook that had been presented to him by Tulsa Torrent at a

170

testimonial dinner honoring his contributions to American forestry.

It was probably time, now, he decided, to call for help from surrounding fire departments. The fire through the forest should be out of control, too late for anybody to do anything about.

Joey Webb should be dead and the copa-ibas destroyed: and he on his way to being a very wealthy, very retired man.

It had all started that night when that bitch Webenhaus had made fun of his lovemaking. She had laughed at him. He had killed her husband and was going to kill her, but those goddamn Indians interrupted. He had been lucky to escape with his own life. And the baby Joey had survived, somehow, too.

There had been all those years of work with the copa-ibas, work that seemed that it would never be successful, and there had been all the money from the Association—which wanted to make sure that the copa-ibas never grew in the United States.

It was a shame, he thought, that he had to share any glory with anyone else from the Association. Stacy looked at the golden hook in his hands. It was a solid-steel bar, almost two feet long, bent into a square handle at one end, curved and razor-sharpened into a hook at the the other end. And even though it was plated thickly with gold, it was still a deadly weapon.

He laughed inwardly. Perhaps he would present it to the other member of the Association as a gift. Right in the neck. The Association appreciated ruthlessness in its people, and such an act might put him on the right track with them. Who knew—he was still only 45—there might be a second, more exciting career awaiting him in life.

"Stacy," a voice said. "It's all over."

He looked up to see Remo O'Sylvan and the old Oriental. He smiled at them, but his mind boiled. Why were they alive? How?

"I didn't hear you come in," he said.

"You didn't expect us either, did you?" Remo said.

"What are you talking about?" he said.

"The fire you set," said Remo.

"Fire? What fire? Our trees?" He jumped up and ran to the window. He had hoped to see the forest still full of flame, but instead, the rim of the valley showed only a thin line of flame around it, the fire having been unable to jump the thick firebreak Remo and Chiun had built.

"The copa-ibas?" Stacy said, his mind moving fast, looking for answers.

"Can it," Remo said. "Who paid you to stop the project? To kill Joey?"

"I don't know what you're talking about," Stacy said. He walked back and sat in his chair. "And if you're going to talk crazy, you can get out. I've got to get the fire departments here." He was sweating now, and the churning of his body was pumping off the smell of his after-shave lotion, a heavy musky smell.

He reached for the telephone. Remo slapped his hand away and gently pushed the chair Stacy was in. It began to whirl around. Remo pushed again. Stacy whirled faster. He thought he was going to throw up. He began to lose his peripheral vision. His sight took on a red tinge. All he could see was Remo's face. Faster and faster he whirled.

Stacy raised the hook and swung at Remo. Somehow he missed. His chair was slowing down. He was facing

172

the old Oriental. He moved the hook back again and swung at the old man.

The last thing Roger Stacy ever saw was Chiun fluttering his hands delicately, slowly, at him, and the golden hook traveling in a long powerful arc, past the old man and back toward himself.

The hook caught Stacy below the Adam's apple and ripped upward, coming to rest in the roof of his mouth.

Roger Stacy fell forward and whimpered, as the blood and the life ran out of him.

Remo stood up from the edge of the desk where he had been perched. "Case closed," he said.

"Not so," said Chiun.

"No?" said Remo. "Smell that after-shave? That's that sweet smell we've been smelling every time there's a body," he said.

"No," Chiun said. "It is similar, but it isn't the same."

CHAPTER SEVENTEEN

Remo didn't trust himself to deal with small-town bureaucracies, so he called Smith and told him to do whatever was necessary to get local fire departments to respond to the burning forests of Tulsa Torrent.

Then he sent Chiun back to Alpha Camp to protect Joey Webb.

And then he drove down the road toward the main camp of the Mountain High Society. Something had been nibbling at his mind for the last thirty hours, and he had finally remembered what it was.

The society's camp was rapidly emptying. The police were letting the protesters leave, a few at a time, and then shuffling them down the road back toward town, under police escort, away from Tulsa Torrent land.

The police were occupied with the protesters when Remo arrived, and he was able to slip into Cicely Winston-Alright's trailer without being challenged.

Her butchered body had been covered with a large blanket. But on a little stand in her room, he found what he was looking for. It was a box and inside was a picture.

When he had made love earlier to the woman, she had said, "Only one man" and pointed to the box.

The picture was signed, "To CeCe. With eternal

love. Lance." Lance Alright. Her last husband. Remo looked at the picture. The bland, blue eyes of Harvey Quibble stared back at him.

He shoved the picture into his trouser pocket. Eight minutes later, he was back at Alpha Camp. He could see fire-fighting apparatus, some painted yellow, some painted red, on the narrow roads leading through the forests, moving up the trails and pumping water on the fire, which now gave signs of burning itself out.

As he went into the Alpha Camp clearing, he saw Chiun. Chiun raised his finger to his mouth to shush Remo, and the younger man walked up silently toward his mentor.

Chiun pointed toward the igloo. Remo could hear voices inside. There was Joey's and there was Harvey Quibble's.

"Why?" Joey was asking.

"It's a long story," Quibble said. His little pip-squeak's voice sounded different now, strong and in control.

"Tell me about it," Joey said.

"I guess there's no reason why not," Quibble said. "I've won and you've lost, and I'll be out of here soon." He paused. "I was married to Cicely. She was involved in this Mountain High stuff. I invested her money for her. Then we went broke. Investments went sour and we had nothing."

"So? That happens to a lot of people," Joey said.

"Not to our kind of people. We loved each other, but we couldn't love each other poor. Fortunately, I knew people in the Middle East in the oil business, and they had heard of the your copa-iba project. It terrified them, the idea of America being self-sufficient with oil. They started a group called the Association, whose whole purpose was to sabotage the project. Cicely and I got divorced; that made it easier for me to take a new identity and get back here as a federal employee, thanks to some helpful congressmen."

"But why the killings?" asked Joey.

"We just wanted to mess up the project, make it too expensive for Tulsa Torrent to continue with," Quibble said. "We never thought that you'd find a way to germinate those seeds and grow them rapidly."

"That shows how little you know," Joey said. "We've found a way to grow them now in any climate. You've lost, Quibble."

"Not really," Quibble said. "Because you'll be dead, and that'll be that. Your secret will go with you."

"We'll see," Joey said stubbornly.

"It's already been taken care of," Quibble said confidently. "That fool Stacy had already notified the company of his decision that this project should be halted as nonproductive. And after I dispose of you, I'm just going to go over and turn off the heaters on the copaibas. In all this confusion, before anybody notices it, the trees will be dead from the cold."

Remo spoke up, loudly.

"The only thing dead is Stacy," he said. He heard a scurrying inside the igloo, and then Harvey Quibble came out through the large opening.

He held a big automatic in his hand.

"You," he said, with a small smile. "Well, well, I have all the troublemakers in one spot."

"It's all over, Quibble. Or should I say Lance?"

"When did you know?"

"Just a while ago. It was your after-shave that tipped us. That smell was everywhere we found a body. And

177

Cicely still had your picture in her bedroom. Tell me, how does it feel to order your own wife murdered?"

"Ex-wife." Quibble said. "She had to go, for the good of the program. We needed a martyr."

"And Pierre LaRue?" Remo asked.

"We needed a scapegoat," Quibble said evenly.

"How'd you kill Carpathian?" Remo asked.

"An injection. I was afraid if you got to him, he'd talk," Quibble said. "How did you get on to me?"

"You made a mistake when you left that tape recorder in the snow," Remo said. "A federal tape recorder. And you're the only federal employee around here. I should have known that sooner."

"Actually, I never expected you to find it," Quibble said. "I thought it would just stay buried under the snow. But, all's well that end's well," he said.

He began to back away from Remo and Chiun to give himself more safe shooting room. His hand was steady as he held the gun on them. But as he moved backward, past the opening to the igloo, Joey reached out, grabbed his heel, and Quibble fell to the snow-covered ground. The gun squirted out of his hands in Remo's direction. Quibble got up, looked at the gun, at Remo, then turned and ran, heading into the forest.

Remo watched him for a moment. Then his eyes lit on Pierre LaRue's double-bladed axe, buried deep in the tree where Remo had thrown it.

Remo yanked the axe from the tree. He raised it over his head and then threw it forward with his right hand. The heavy handle of the axe whistled as it turned over and over again. The blade of the tool buried itself deep into Harvey Quibble's back. He fell to the ground with a whooshing exhalation of air.

"Timber," mumbled Remo under his breath, as he watched the man fall.

Joey Webb came out of the igloo and stood with Remo and Chiun.

Chiun looked around at the trees, at the brightly starred sky and said, "This is beautiful. I think I will go up into the woods to commune with nature. Just me and the outdoors, sharing the oneness of life."

"Carry your own trunks," Remo said.

CHAPTER EIGHTEEN

Chiun had marched off into the woods, to find some peace and quiet.

Remo had called Smith again, while Joey was in the back of the log cabin.

"I just traced that tape recorder to Harvey Quibble," Smith said.

"I know all about it," Remo said. "He's dead. Stacy's dead. The job's done."

"Oh," said Smith. "Then I guess there isn't much for us to talk about, is there?"

"No," Remo said.

He heard Smith clear his throat, nervously, as if trying to muster up the courage to speak.

"What is it?" Remo said.

"Give Joey . . . give Joey my love."

Remo looked up as the pretty long-legged woman walked toward him. She had taken off her clothes. She extended her long, naked arms toward him.

"I'll be glad to," Remo said. "Glad to."

And he was.

Warren Murphy

More bestselling action/adventure from Pinnacle, America's #1 series publisher. Over 14 million copies of THE DESTROYER in print!